Abby's Road

Susie Feickert

ISBN: 979-8-89316-816-7 - Paperback
ISBN: 979-8-89316-815-0 - eBook
ISBN: 979-8-89316-817-4 - Hardcover

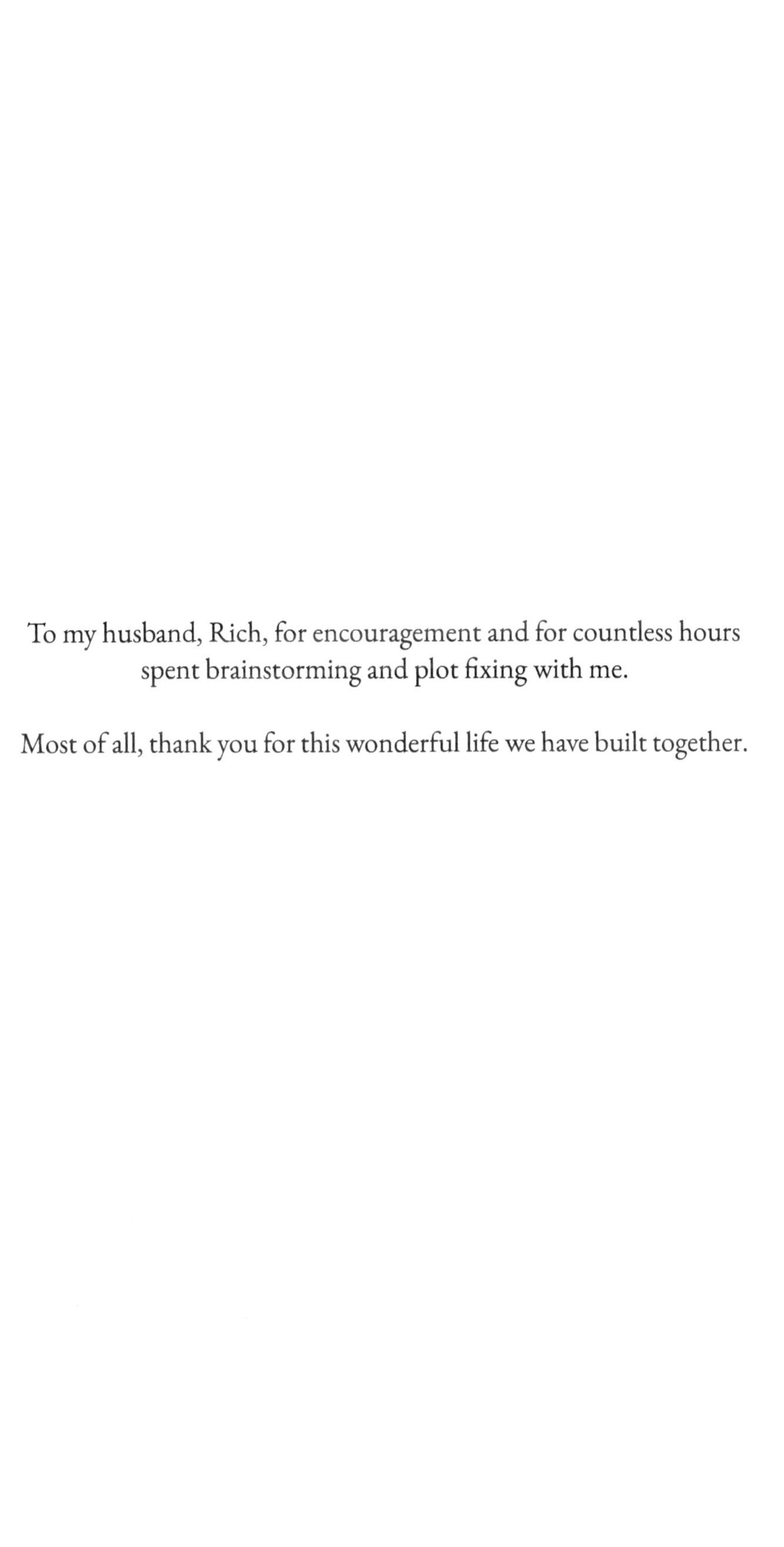

To my husband, Rich, for encouragement and for countless hours spent brainstorming and plot fixing with me.

Most of all, thank you for this wonderful life we have built together.

Prologue

Having grabbed a bucket of warm soapy water and stooping down to clean my horse's swollen sheath, he picked up his back leg closest to me and stretched it out. Copper was my first horse, and this was not our first rodeo. For anyone who does not know, the sheath is the opening in the horse's underbelly where his penis comes out of and retracts into. Sometimes horses get what our vet likes to refer to as "beans up in there," and it causes irritation. The beans are really nothing more than clumped dirt. The solution is to get some warm soapy water and reach way up in there to clean the beans out. I mean way up there, like up to your elbow. I have done this with Copper a handful of times, and he now knows what to expect. We developed a strong mutual trust in each other years ago. This time, however, there did not seem to be many beans up there. I cleaned it as best I could and decided to give it a day or so to see what happened.

The next morning, Copper's sheath was even more swollen. I called our vet, and he was out within an hour, which is one of the perks of living in a small rural town in the mountains of north Idaho. He spent about one minute with Copper and said, "Oh yeah, I know what this is. How old is he again?"

"He's twenty-eight," I replied.

"Come here and feel this," Dr. Derek said.

His sheath was noticeably cold. We had had an exceptionally cold winter and the nights were still below freezing. Dr. Derek explained that this condition was due to a lack of blood flow. It is no different from an older person sitting on a plane all day, causing their legs to swell up some.

"The absolute best thing in the world for this is massaging it."

"What?"

"Yep. Watch this."

Dr. Derek rubbed it for about thirty seconds, and it felt warmer. We just needed to help get the blood circulating there. If we didn't, the tissue could become necrotic and die; then it becomes necessary to amputate part of it, and it's a real mess.

"You only need to do this about three to four times a day. Don't worry about the middle of the night. And as soon as the nights warm up, this will stop."

"Does it hurt him to do this?"

"Ah hell no. He likes it," was Dr. Derek's response as he walked back to his truck.

Dr. Derek is the only veterinarian in our town and exactly how you would imagine a small-town vet. He is in his late fifties, early sixties, and treats large and small animals as if they were his own. He prefers making house calls when he can, especially when it comes time to put a dog down. He claims it is much easier and less stressful for everyone, especially the dog. He is an excellent doctor with a dry sense of humor. Everyone in town has his home phone number and loves him. Dr. Derek has even been spotted on the side of the road, outside of his vet truck, after delivering calves, stripping down to his skivvies in early spring, and hosing himself off before going on to his next appointment.

It was early March, and the daytime temperatures had been hovering in the high thirties for two weeks. I was beyond ready for spring. Since moving here from Virginia in 2015, every year at that time, I started to feel that old familiar longing for warm breezes, sun on my face, the smell of freshly cut grass, and garden dirt ready for some attention. I am not sure I will ever get used to the longer winters here. The perfect summer weather with no humidity, daytime temps in the eighties, and nighttime temps in the fifties are what keep us here. That and the jaw-dropping views of the majestic mountains from just about anywhere in our county, especially from our property.

As Dr. Derek drove out of the driveway, my dad and my husband came walking around the barn.

"What's going on?" Lucas asked.

I explained to him what had happened and what Dr. Derek had said. Since my dad and Lucas help with feeding and caring for the horses, I told them that massaging Copper's sheath should be done several times each day. The two exchanged looks, and then my dad said, with a grin on his face, "Abby, I don't mind helping you feed the horses, but I am not doing that."

"Me either," Lucas said with a laugh. "He already likes me enough."

"Really, guys? This is my horse and I would do anything for him. It's no big deal."

After turning Copper back out, I walked the length of the horse field before heading home. Having just introduced a fifth horse to our herd three days prior, they were going through a reorganizing of the pecking order. This resulted in a lot of chasing the new guy around the pasture and, unfortunately, nine stitches in his back leg. Other than Copper's current ailment, all seemed quiet at the moment and I prayed it would stay that way.

As I walked back to the house, past the chicken coop, a bald eagle flew out of a tree not twenty feet from me. I watched him soar over our property, into the valley with the Kootenai River running down the middle of it, and toward the adjacent snow-topped mountains. The clear sky was a deep shade of blue—a completely different color of blue from the Virginia sky where I had spent most of my life. The air was crisp, and except for the occasional clucking of the chickens, it was completely silent. There are no cars or sirens and no neighbors within a mile. We rarely even have airplanes fly over us. Over the last eight years, I have come to love living in north Idaho and cannot imagine ever moving back to the suburbs of Washington, DC.

It was only ten years ago that I was living in a country club neighborhood in Haymarket, Virginia, appreciating a rich social life revolving around the club, raising our teenage boys, Billy and Kevin, and enjoying a successful career in corporate sales. We had a maid and a live-in au pair. I am sure it was a lifestyle many people would love to have.

My full life all came crashing down one day when my husband of twenty years decided he was in love with someone else and asked for a divorce.

I now live on an eighty-acre farm in a small agricultural county in Bonners Ferry, Idaho, twelve miles from the Canadian border, with Lucas, my second husband. When I say small, I mean 12,500 people and one stop light in the entire county. We are surrounded by mountains and wilderness and every type of wildlife you can imagine. This area of the country is stunningly gorgeous.

Initially, this way of life was completely foreign to me. It was a real eye-opener and a far cry from my East Coast lifestyle. There are people here who respect and often choose to live simpler lives or off the land—reminiscent of the pioneer days in America. To say I experienced an initial culture shock is an understatement. The laid-back atmosphere took some getting used to. In the process, I have unexpectedly developed a deep respect and awe for the people here, especially the women, who continue to amaze me. Their strength and fortitude is unwavering. I have often wondered if I will ever be able to completely assimilate into this wonderful and challenging culture.

How did I get here? It all started after my divorce and with Match.com.

1

Lucas

I arrived at the coffee shop in town with what my grandmother used to refer to as collywobbles in my stomach. I remembered her telling me she had collywobbles when she first met my grandfather. This was the first time I had experienced those since my divorce. Ugh! It made me feel a little unsettled and slightly nauseous. A million thoughts raced through my head. Since spending a great deal of time emailing back and forth on Match.com, Lucas and I were getting to know each other well. I had started to really like his personality. He was funny and very witty. Family seemed to be of utmost importance to him. If there were truly any loyal men left in this world, he seemed like he may be one. However, I wasn't sure if we would have chemistry. I suddenly realized I had high hopes for this meeting and would be disappointed if I didn't find him attractive. What if he didn't find me attractive?

Joining a dating website in 2010 is not something I ever intended to do. However, one of my close friends convinced me to give it a try. She had been divorced a year longer than me and assured me, if nothing else, it would be entertaining. She was right.

My first two lunch dates, with different guys, were spent listening to these gentlemen's health ailments. My entire second lunch date conversation revolved around my date's diverticulitis. I'm not sure what type of vibe I was giving off that made these men want to divulge their entire medical histories to me within the first hour of our meeting. In addition, after my first lunch date, date #1 called and wanted to know if I would be interested in seeing his goldfish collection. Not tropical, rare fish, but goldfish. I did not have high hopes for this dating app. I did, however, stick with it a little longer.

When Lucas and I started communicating, we emailed back and forth for about a month. From what I could tell by his profile photo, he was very handsome. He was six feet one, one eighty-five, and five years older than me. Lucas had gotten divorced three years earlier than me and had four kids between the ages of thirty-two and twenty-one. He lived on a farm in Purcellville, Virginia, not too far from me. Compared to most of the other men on those dating websites, he certainly seemed to most closely resemble what I was looking for.

Surprisingly, and yet still skeptical, I found myself looking forward to his prompt early morning emails. He emailed every morning like clockwork, and I responded. I started to wake up every morning and reach for my phone before I got out of bed. I was enjoying this. Our texts were blunt and honest; therefore, we really got to know each other, as much as possible with just emails.

One morning, his email contained a proposal of sorts. He proposed that we meet for coffee and spend one hour together. No more and no less. At the end of the hour, we would leave without any mention of anything in the future. Apparently, we both had experienced a few dates that were hard to end. I thought about it for a few minutes and realized that the deal worked for me also. I agreed.

Lucas was waiting out front for me. We recognized each other from our photos online. He was even more handsome in person, taller than I expected, and had the athletic build of a man who clearly worked out. His dark wavy hair and goatee gave him a hint of that bad boy look, which I found very attractive. He was wearing jeans and a golf shirt and carried an air of confidence, not to be confused with cockiness, which was most appealing.

Lucas grabbed our coffees, and we sat at a corner table of the coffee shop furthest away from the door. I was pleasantly surprised at how easily our conversation flowed. There never seemed to be any lack of things to discuss. I am not a shy person but, like my parents, am normally very guarded and reserved, especially when I first meet someone. Somehow Lucas made it easy for me to open up.

We talked about family and how important it is to both of us. We talked about things we enjoyed doing and about how we wanted the second half of our lives to unfold. He was looking for a life partner to have adventures with. Lucas wanted to make the most of the rest of his life. He wanted to try new things and live in new places. His sense of adventure and the idea of living in the country, raising cattle, and riding horses appealed to me. I was ready for something different and liked the idea of making the most out of the second half of our lives. At the end of the hour, which seemed to fly by, we parted ways with no discussion about anything in the future. I kind of liked this guy and hoped he felt the same about me.

· · · · ●· ● · ● · ·

Later that evening, Lucas texted me and asked if I would be interested in going out to lunch. I replied that I would but wanted to know what the rules for the second date were. He told me he didn't know because he had not had a second date yet. That made me chuckle.

Our second date was wonderful. He picked me up at my house, and we had lunch in The Plains and drove out to the large cattle ranch Lucas managed years earlier. He gave me a tour of the entire place, and I learned a few things about raising cattle. We spent the entire afternoon together. I was becoming completely enamored with Lucas and his life. I knew nothing about farm life. At the same time, I was super intrigued by it.

· · · · ●· ● · ● · ·

Until then, my life had been spent living in a suburb of Washington, DC, which was a great place to raise Billy and Kevin. They went to private school. We had a live-in au pair and a maid, all very similar to my childhood. When not working, most of my time centered around the boys' sporting events or cooking for a house full of boys most weekends. I volunteered at their school as much as possible. When time allowed, I also loved playing tennis and golf. I loved that part of my life.

As time went on, that marriage became more estranged. My husband was spending less time at home with us and more time after hours at his office. We were both busy. Me with work and the boys and him at his office doing God knows what all those late hours. I suppose it should not have been a complete surprise when, after twenty years together, he announced that he was leaving me for someone else.

Well aware of my first husband's flaws, I knew I needed something/someone completely different. Loyalty and commitment are paramount to me. Trusting someone is not something that comes quickly or easily for me. I have always been this way—a trait that the divorce enhanced. I wanted a partner in every way, and I needed to laugh more. In addition, for years I had been saying to my friends, as they would later remind me, that I should be living on a farm somewhere. I would like that. They remembered me saying it a lot more than I remember saying it. Even though I had never really ridden a horse, except for the occasional nose-to-tail trail ride, I kept trying to get them to go on a Dude Ranch vacation with me, to no avail.

For our third date, Lucas invited me to his house for dinner. The idea of going to his house made me a little nervous. I contemplated going online, paying the fee, and looking Lucas up to see if he had any previous arrest records but then told myself I was being ridiculous. I needed to think this through, given where I had come from in my first marriage. I had lived a pretty pampered lifestyle and wasn't sure I could envision the same lifestyle with Lucas. He was completely different from my ex-husband, which is also what I wanted. The part that concerned me was that not obly was Lucas different but so was his lifestyle. At least, that is what I surmised after only two dates. I concluded that I needed to give this a little more time and keep an open mind.

2

A Turning Point

I knew he lived in the country but was not prepared for how far out it was. On that long drive to Lucas's house that night, I started to think about how much I knew about him. I was no longer twenty-something years old. At forty-eight, I always thought of myself as having a lot of common sense and being a good judge of character. If I had had a daughter, I may have told her that going to a guy's house in the middle of nowhere for dinner on the third date wasn't the brightest idea. In addition, I was wrestling with the idea of what a life with Lucas would look like and if it would be enough for me. What did I really want in a relationship? Sometimes I wasn't so sure. However, something about Lucas drew me to him.

After about an hour on dark gravel roads, I arrived at his driveway and could not see the house from the road. It had taken much longer to get there than I expected, and I was immediately struck with a bolt of apprehension. I knew I had been out of the dating scene for twenty years, but I had seen all those Datelines, and you never know who you may be dealing with. I was in the middle of the most rural part of Loudon County with no other houses in sight. I felt completely isolated. Part of me wanted to turn the car around and just drive home.

Instead, I called my mother and told her about my sudden bout of cold feet. She was quiet for a minute and then said she thought I was okay. My mother always erred on the side of caution in everything in life. She was nervous about everything. In fact, we had nicknamed her 'Nervous Nellie,' although she never knew that. For some reason unknown to me, she thought this was okay. I didn't question her. I was looking for a reason to move forward despite my fear. I hung up the phone and continued up the driveway. I still felt a mix of butterflies and wanted to be smart about this; I was in unfamiliar territory.

I knew Lucas had a one-hundred-fifty-acre farm in Purcellville; his ex-wife still lived in the big house, and he lived in the older smaller house. He used to have cattle there, and it was where he had raised his kids. That was the extent of what I knew about his farm. I had no idea what to expect.

About a quarter of a mile up the driveway, Lucas's house was on the right. It looked like an old farmhouse from the early 1900s. It was a small, two-story white house with a red metal roof and a large covered front porch with a porch swing. It was quite idyllic and inviting, like a painting of older and simpler days. There didn't seem to be any curtains or blinds in any of the windows, allowing me to see Lucas standing in what I supposed was the kitchen. I could see a fenced garden across the driveway from the house, and everything around the house seemed to be well taken care of. The field on the other side of the garden had several large round bales of hay in it from what I could see in the dark.

I parked the car and sat wondering which door I should go to—the front door or the one on the side, which appeared to get more use due to its convenience. I didn't wonder for long because Lucas opened the side door and came out to greet me.

"You made it."

He reached over to hug me. *If he only knew how close I came to bailing.* Instantly I felt glad I had not.

"Yes. Although I had no idea you were this far out on gravel roads. I bet it is a pretty drive in the daytime."

Virginia is known for its very picturesque rolling countryside. Between all the vineyards and the equine hunt country, there is nothing that compares to it.

We walked into the house through a large mud room and then into the kitchen. It was a spacious kitchen with a linoleum floor and older cabinets and countertops. It didn't have the trendy granite countertops or the tile or wood floor that I was used to. However, everything was immaculate. There was a good-sized oak kitchen table off to one side and a small antique hutch/jelly cabinet against the opposing wall. The kitchen opened to the family room, which had a leather couch and recliner, a TV, and a natural wood corner cabinet that looked like it had been made of different types of wood. When I asked about it, Lucas humbly told me that he had made it out of scraps. I thought it was pretty and unique. There was so much detail in it, I couldn't believe he made it. There was a bathroom and bedroom on the main floor and four bedrooms and a bathroom upstairs. The basement was half the footprint of the house, with only a washer and dryer in it.

Lucas told me the house his ex-wife lived in, further down the driveway, was newer and that he built it. He said that house had all the upgrades in it and was almost seven thousand square feet, which sounded huge, considering I raised my kids in a six thousand-square-foot house and that felt more than big enough. Somehow that made me feel a little better about a possible future together. Once they separated, Lucas partially gutted and rebuilt his current house. After Lucas retired, he got involved with a local charity, building houses for the poor. In addition, he had built several houses for his own family while his kids were growing up. He never built houses as a profession but had gotten good at it and enjoyed it. Apparently, there was nothing he could not fix or build. I could also tell by the way he finished things that he was a perfectionist.

Together we cooked a dinner of stuffed shells, salad, and garlic bread that night while sipping on wine. He had a way of making me laugh no matter what we were doing. My butterflies were finally subsiding. When he asked me what I thought of his house, the first thing that came to my mind was why there weren't curtains or blinds at any of the windows. Lucas chuckled and asked why he would need them. There were no neighbors anywhere close. I couldn't argue with that theory, although I still felt strange—like we were exposed to whatever was outside lurking in the bushes.

My father grew up in Baltimore City, and even when he moved us to the country when my brother and I were little, he never stopped his daily routine of going through the house just before dinner every single evening and closing all of the drapes and blinds. I must have adopted this ritual from him since I also do the same.

I enjoyed Lucas's quick wit and quirky sense of humor, which we seemed to share. There was also something about him that I found so attractive. I wasn't sure if it was his confidence, his looks, or the easy laid-back way he seemed to handle me, which made me feel safe. Maybe it was a combination. Regardless, I was starting to develop real feelings for this guy. At the same time, I still had that little voice in my head wondering if I could be happy with him. I had such mixed emotions.

I didn't stay too late due to the looming long ride home on back gravel roads. As I was leaving, Lucas walked me out to my car and gave me my first real kiss since meeting him. Well, damn, those butterflies were back. As I pulled out of his driveway, I was feeling almost giddy with happiness for the first time since my divorce. On the ride home, I thought how very glad I was that I had not bailed on this date at the foot of his driveway.

· · ● · ● · ● · ·

Over the next month and a half, Lucas and I continued dating and enjoying each other's company. At this point, I was back working and Lucas was lucky enough to have had a very successful business, which allowed him to retire at forty-four. He was now fifty-three and volunteered as an EMT and for Habitat for Humanity and Project Mend a House among other assorted positions. I admired the fact that he was so dedicated to volunteering for worthy causes. I decided to have him over for dinner to meet my boys. We were getting to that point, and things were starting to get serious with us.

I had planned on making a chicken dish, until a good friend told me, in no uncertain terms, that I absolutely could not serve a new beau chicken the first time I had him over for dinner. She insisted I make prime rib. I wasn't sure it mattered but felt it wouldn't hurt to heed her advice this time.

That Thursday, as I was preparing prime rib, twice-baked potatoes, and a Caesar salad for dinner, Billy and Kevin walked in the door, from throwing the lacrosse ball out front, with Lucas. Lucas had come right from work and was still wearing his EMT uniform. The three of them had already met in the front yard and were talking up a storm. I could barely get a word in. At the same time, I was thrilled they were all getting along so well. They talked about lacrosse. Lucas's boys had also played. They talked about school and what it was like to work as an EMT. They talked about the Redskins. Having owned a gym business in Herndon, Lucas personally knew several of the players, and my boys seemed thoroughly impressed. Their conversations continued all through dinner. Lucas seemed completely engrossed in Billy and Kevin's lives, and they seemed equally as interested in his.

As soon as we finished eating, I remember feeling like that evening could not have gone any better when Lucas looked at Billy and Kevin and said, "Hey, guys. Since your mom made this incredible dinner, how about the three of us clean up?"

I held my breath, wondering how the boys would respond to Lucas suggesting they do a chore, even if it was with him. Would they be put off by him suggesting that? After all, Lucas was not their father. Since the divorce, I had never asked Billy or Kevin to help clean up the kitchen, nor did they ever offer. In hindsight, maybe I should have. Instead, I felt so sorry for them going through our divorce that I took on every task I could for them. My guilt was overwhelming at times, even if it had not been all my fault, and it seemed to cloud the bigger picture.

"Okay," said Kevin. Billy also got up to help.

As they started clearing the plates, I was in unfamiliar territory and very unsure of how to proceed at that moment. Should I help? I certainly didn't want to ruin a good thing. Not knowing what else to do, I excused myself and went to the bathroom. After closing the door, I stood in front of the sink, took a couple of big breaths, and tried to let all these new emotions settle down. In the grand scheme of things, Lucas's gesture of getting the boys to help him clean up the kitchen may have seemed small, but it had been huge to me. It had been a perfect evening.

Once Lucas left, Billy and Kevin approached me with smiles.

"He's got about the biggest arms I have ever seen!" Kevin exclaimed.

"Mom, he drives a light blue Prius," Billy said, grinning.

To which I replied, "I know, and he couldn't care less what people think."

We all laughed. So far, so good. Everything seemed to be going well.

$$\cdots\bullet\cdot\bullet\cdot\bullet\cdot\cdots$$

The following weekend, I was at Lucas's house early on a Saturday when one of his neighbors called and asked if we could help him sort cattle.

"Hang on Sam. Abby, do you want to go and sort cattle this morning?"

"Sure," I replied, somewhat oblivious to what exactly that meant. If I was going to consider changing my lifestyle, I may as well jump right in. How hard can this be?

I suppose I am the epitome of the "city girl" who loves animals and knows next to nothing about most of them but will never admit that. Deep down, I knew I had a lot to learn.

Once we arrived at Sam's farm, there were about one-hundred-eighty head of cows and calves. Our job was to separate the cows from their calves, run the calves through the chute, vaccinate and ear tag them. We did not do this on horseback like I had seen in the movies. We did this on foot, carrying what looked like plastic canoe paddles. As we started separating them, I could not help but feel sorry for the moms, who were clearly upset at what we were doing with their babies. However, I wasn't going to show any weakness here. I would keep that to myself and do my job. I knew enough to know there was a good difference between how people viewed their pet dogs, and cats, and how farmers viewed their livestock.

At one point, there were about eight to ten cows, visibly upset, looking like they were going to charge the gate at any moment. I walked out in front of them with my paddle to keep them from stampeding the gate. I guess I thought they would back down from me. The next thing I knew, Lucas grabbed my shoulder and pulled me out of the way of the herd as they rushed toward the gate, totally ignoring me and seemingly happy to run me over.

"Abby, you have got to be more careful. They can really hurt you."

"Thanks," I replied, somewhat bewildered. That had been a close call. It seemed I was going to need to be both brave and smart.

Once we were done with the cattle, Sam told us that he had shot a bunch of geese earlier and asked if we wanted to help him breast them. Lucas looked at me as if asking if that would be okay. Oddly, I felt like I was somehow being tested. Wanting to show him I had grit and not one to normally back down from a challenge, I said, "Sure."

Sorting the cattle had not gone too bad. Other than almost getting run over, I seemed to have held my own. Maybe this was a chance to redeem myself a little.

I am not sure what I was thinking, or expecting. When we walked around the back of the house, there was a pile of approximately twenty dead geese. *Oh Lord, I hope I can do this.* They were much larger than I expected, but then I had never been this close to a goose. I know I am not capable of killing an animal, but these were already dead. *Not that different from cutting up a whole chicken that you buy in the supermarket, right? Only with the feathers and head still attached.* I would keep telling myself that.

Sam handed me a knife. Lucas and Sam each picked up a goose and got to work. I was completely out of my comfort zone. Nevertheless, I picked up a goose and started to follow what Lucas was doing. As soon as I made that first cut, there was this overpowering stench of what I can only describe as "death" that made me want to wretch up everything I had eaten for breakfast and all three meals from the day before. Lucas looked over at me and asked, "What's wrong? Are you okay? You don't look so good."

He said all of this with the hint of a smirk on his face like he was half expecting that reaction out of me. That made me so mad, I wanted to hit him with my dissected goose. The fleeting thought of the entire bloody innards of my goose spilling down the front of Lucas was the icing on the cake. At the last minute, I turned my head and gagged several times. Thankful I hadn't lost my breakfast. I handed Lucas my knife and walked into the house. I was sure I heard them both chuckling as I left. However, Lucas never said another word about that incident, and I was glad.

· · · · ● · ● · · · ·

I think he was feeling a little bad for putting me in that situation when he invited me to go fishing a few days later. Ah, this was something much easier that anyone could do. Not too hard to stand with a line in the water. On a warm, yet cloudy, humid afternoon, we went to a pond on his neighbor's farm. We stood about twenty feet apart when we started. Lucas insisted I bait my own hook. That was okay. Nothing could be worse than breasting a goose. I punched my hook through that wriggly worm and whispered, "I did it" to myself. Within five minutes, Lucas had a fish. Within ten minutes, he had another. Within thirty minutes, he had several and all I managed to catch were sticks from the bottom of the pond. As my competitive spirit started to kick in, I got increasingly frustrated.

"Lucas, this is lame. What else do you country boys do?" I snapped.

He looked at me and grinned again as if he was so much better than me. Nonetheless, I kept my composure and bided my time until we were finished fishing.

We went back to his house for dinner and while sitting on the front porch, Lucas asked me if I had ever shot a gun.

"Sure. One time I shot a policeman's gun at a target." Although I did not remember much about that event. It was years ago.

"Have you ever shot a shotgun?"

"No."

"Do you think you could hit that hay bale with one?" He was pointing at a large round hay bale about thirty yards away from us.

"Probably," I said somewhat confidently. It wasn't that far away. How could I miss it?

Lucas went into the house and came out with a loaded shot gun. He handed me the gun and ear protection.

"Do I really need ear protection?"

"I would suggest it."

I put the ear protection on and held the gun up, like I thought I was supposed to, then put it down and turned to look at Lucas, who was standing behind me with his fingers in his ears and his eyes scrunched closed, like a toddler who didn't want to be reprimanded. Seriously? I turned back around again. *How hard can this be?* I aimed and pulled the trigger.

The next thing I knew I was clear on the other side of the porch, half standing and half on the ground. Lucas had caught me before I went all the way down and cracked my head on the rail. My shoulder was screaming in pain.

"Are you okay?" asked Lucas.

"I think so. Damn, my shoulder hurts. Did I hit it?"

"I don't think so," Lucas said with that same darn smirk on his face. "But, it was a good try."

That was it. I was planning the next date, and it would be something I was good at. It was time to turn the tables a little bit.

· · · • · • · • · ·

Lucas agreed to bike part of the Mt. Vernon trail with me. I had recently done several triathlons, and biking was one of my favorite activities. Lucas lived close to the Mt. Vernon trail in Purcellville. I showed up at his house on Saturday morning with my decked-out, $3,000 Canyon Speedmax bike and dressed in my bike outfit and clip-in shoes. I was used to riding twenty-five to forty miles with other bikers several times a week and loved it.

I am not sure what I expected, but Lucas was standing there in jean shorts and a tee shirt with a very old green, dusty, rusty five-speed Schwinn bike. I asked where he got it.

"In the rafters of the barn," replied Lucas as if it had been there for fifty years, which it may well have been.

As Lucas threw the bikes into the back of his pickup truck, I cringed at the thought of my bike getting messed up but thought it best not to say anything. I was finally feeling confident about doing something with Lucas where I was positive I could hold my own.

Once we got to the trailhead with the bikes, Lucas noticed his derailer was broken. Being as resourceful as he is, Lucas grabbed a stick and jammed it into the derailer to keep it in at least one gear. That eight-inch stick stuck out of the side of his bike for our entire ride. Now I was the one chuckling.

At the end of the day, we rode twenty-five miles on the trail and Lucas, even though he only had one gear, managed to keep up with me the whole time. He never complained once. I am not sure which one of us is more competitive. However, we are both game for anything, and that has the potential to make our lives fun.

· · · ● · ● · ● · ·

A couple of months after we started dating, Lucas took me to Harpers Ferry, W. VA for lunch on the back of his Harley Davidson motorcycle. Motorcycles have always scared me, and I had never ridden on one.

When I was in college, I did a brief internship with a county state attorney's office in Maryland. I sat in on one trial that involved two fatalities in a motorcycle accident. I recalled seeing photographs of brain matter on a guard rail. That had always stuck with me, and I had never wanted to get on a motorcycle since.

This was a bright red Harley with black leather saddlebags with long black fringe. It was in excellent condition. All the chrome looked like it had just been polished. It was pristine and looked like it belonged in a Hell's Angels group. Lucas could feel I was nervous and tried to reassure me we would be okay. He had a way of doing that, that no one else ever had.

The entire trip was on back roads in parts of Virginia and West Virginia that I had never seen. It was incredibly scenic, but the faster we went, the more scared I got. I kept thinking of all the catastrophic accidents that could occur should an animal jump out in front of us. What if we hit wet pavement and the wheels slid out from under us? I am sure I had a death grip on Lucas during that first ride, and I am sure he felt it. He would periodically put one hand on my lower leg, as we were riding, which somehow made me feel a little safer.

Once we got to Harper's Ferry and parked, we took off our helmets. That was the first time I noticed the red, white, and blue do-rag on Lucas's head. I must have missed that when we were putting the helmets on. At first, I was not sure what to think of that as I caught myself staring and wanting to laugh a little. My next thought was, *that's kind of hot. It's like a bad boy thing.* I was absolutely starting to fall for this guy. By the end of the day, I started to enjoy the ride. I realized I trusted Lucas, which was huge for me.

Once we got home, I even asked him, "Have you ever participated in Rolling Thunder?"

Rolling Thunder in Washington, DC is a hugely patriotic event. It has grown to be the largest one-day motorcycle event in the country with people coming from every corner of the country to participate. Riders start at the Pentagon parking lot and ride through the Mall area of DC on Memorial Day weekend. Some of the roughest-looking bikers you can imagine show up along with everyone else and ride side by side to commemorate fallen military men and women. It is hard not to get swept up in the emotional display of patriotism at this event.

"I have and am not so sure I would do it again."

"Why?"

"It was an incredibly hot day on the pavement, and we moved at a snail's pace. Why do you ask?"

"I was just thinking I might like to do that someday."

Lucas smiled at me and just shook his head.

· · · • · • · • · ·

On September 24, 2011, eleven months after meeting Lucas at that coffee shop and after both of us declaring we would never get married again, we said our vows in Purcellville, Virginia, in his brother's backyard. We opted for a small, immediate-family-only ceremony, and it was perfect! All of our kids, my two and Lucas's four, were there, some of them meeting for the first time, along with our parents and brothers, sisters, nieces, and nephews. It wasn't the large formal wedding that we had both had in our previous marriages. It was much more quaint and personal. We enjoyed ourselves so much more.

I was committed now to a lifetime of adventure with Lucas—however that may turn out. The one thing I was certain of was a life with Lucas would most likely include horses in some way, and I knew next to nothing about horses.

3

Learning to Horseback Ride

For my birthday that year, Lucas gave me a series of horseback riding lessons. I had always wanted to learn to ride. It just was never an option for our lifestyle. If I was going to plan a life with Lucas, riding was going to be part of it. I needed to do this. *What is learning to ride at forty-eight years old going to be like?* I wondered.

Lucas had always ridden. He had horses when he was growing up. After graduating from college, he managed a very large cattle ranch in Hume for a few years. Riding was part of his daily routine there. He had done a little roping and even tried to ride a rodeo bull one time. In fact, he had owned and ridden horses for most of his life. Lucas was about as close to a cowboy as anyone I had ever met. I was super excited to learn how to ride.

We had been talking about moving somewhere out west and possibly having cattle once my youngest was off at college. I had visions of spending our lives in Montana running a cattle ranch where we'd spend much of our time on horseback, herding cattle, or driving them to various seasonal pastures.

I showed up for my first lesson in Purcellville early one afternoon. My instructor's name was Sharon, and she was a few years older than me. She was shorter than me but striking with her blonde hair, flawless skin, and perfect smile. She had grown up riding and was now married to a bull rider who traveled around competing in rodeos. We got along very well. I enjoyed her as much as I enjoyed time with the horses.

The first lesson consisted of the basics. I was riding a liver chestnut-colored gelding named Edgar. Edgar was quiet and would have been happy to stand still in the arena for the entire hour of our lesson. We went over walking, stopping, turning, and backing up. It was uneventful but fun. I loved it. This was a whole different world for me, and I was eager to see where it took me. Sharon and I talked about the rodeo, and I mentioned that if I ever got good enough, I would love to try barrel racing. Sharon told me that one of their horses was a retired five-time West Virginia barrel champion, and we could work on that some. Okay, I thought, realizing I had so much to learn before we got to that point. However, I went home feeling very enthusiastic about my newly found favorite thing to do.

In my second lesson, I learned to post at the working trot. Again, it was somewhat uneventful, but I loved it. There was just something about being on a horse that seemed to soothe me. I even loved the smell of horses. I could've spent hours in the barn just grooming them and been perfectly content. I couldn't wait until we were living out west and riding all the time.

At my third lesson, Sharon had a barrel course set up in the arena and a completely different horse saddled and ready for me.

"Ah, what are we doing?" I asked apprehensively.

I was not ready to start running barrels. I knew I had a long way to go yet.

"I thought we would get you used to the barrel pattern by just walking and trotting it. This is Mabel—the retired barrel champion I told you about."

Oh boy. Mabel was not too much taller than Edgar, but she was solid muscle, everywhere. She was a beautiful, tobiano paint mare with one blue eye and one brown eye. I was slightly intimidated by her to say the least. Sharon's husband was watching from the small bleachers with a friend of his. I now had an audience. I climbed up on Mabel, immediately feeling the power beneath me as my stomach started to flip-flop.

The first thing Sharon had me do was walk Mabel around the ring twice to warm her up. Then, we trotted her around the ring. She had a much bigger trot than the gelding I was used to, and for the first time, I felt a little fearful. I started to think about falling off. I was pretty high up, and if I fell off her, I would surely injure myself. My other fear was feeling out of control. *What if she took off on me, and I could not stop her? However, we were inside of the ring. How far could we really go?*

Next, we walked the cloverleaf-shaped barrel pattern a few times. Then she asked me to trot it if I was comfortable. *Why not?* I thought immediately. I needed to suppress the fear that was creeping in and just do it. I spurred Mabel into a trot, and we rounded the first barrel, then the second. So far, so good. I was beginning to relax a little, and right before we rounded that third barrel, I let out a relaxing breath.

I will never know what kind of message I sent Mabel at that moment. She turned that last barrel and did what she does best. She took off at a dead sprint to the other side of the arena. When she finally stopped by turning sideways to avoid slamming into the fence, which made me lose my balance a little, I hopped off her so fast, I don't even remember doing it. I have never been so petrified in my life! I was breathing heavily and wincing from the pain in my tailbone, which I was sure was now broken from bouncing so hard on top of Mabel. Sharon's husband was doubled over laughing. All he could say between laughing was, "You should have seen your face. Oh my God."

I wondered if he also laughed at car accidents.

After a minute, Sharon said, "You do know you have to get back on her, right?"

"What? Now? I am pretty sure I cannot sit on anything at this moment."

"It's okay. Take a minute and then you can just ride her back to the barn."

So, I rode her back to the barn, while Sharon led her with the lead line, feeling like a total failure for getting so scared. I could not help it, though. Maybe learning to ride was going to take longer than I thought.

I continued with those lessons, but never got on Mabel again. If I had been a teenager, maybe I would not have been so scared and would have tried Mabel again. I now realize that learning to ride at forty-eight comes with a lot more fear as opposed to learning when you are much younger. That makes it a little slower going. Oh, don't get me wrong, I want to be able to gallop a horse across a field, as fast as they can go. I dream about doing that. I even get chills watching barrel racing and reining competitions because my heart wants to do that so badly. My ultimate dream is to gallop a horse on a beach someday. It is my brain that is overly cautious at times, letting the fear creep in.

After taking a dozen or so lessons from Sharon, Lucas stumbled upon a horse farm in Bealeton that needed help keeping all their horses in shape. He made a deal with the owner, allowing us to ride any of their eighteen horses anytime we wanted. They had a large outdoor arena and were always hosting schooling shows, which I participated in whenever I could. For two years, I spent many hours there riding various horses in their arena and on trail rides. That experience helped me get comfortable with different horses.

I also learned how to put saddles on and tack up a horse, how to pick their feet, and how to groom them. I rode all types of horses. I rode an appaloosa that I absolutely loved. He was super sweet and had not had much training. He and I mostly played with obstacles in the ring. I rode a couple of different Tennessee Walkers. Their gaits were so comfortable that I questioned why anyone would have anything other than a gaited horse. They could move quickly and never bounce you in the saddle. They were so smooth.

I even rode a small Haflinger who had been trained to mostly pull carts. When the owner suggested I try riding him, I questioned if he was big enough for me. I am five feet nine. He was short, more like a pony, but very stocky. They insisted I try. Once I got on him in the ring, I felt like my feet could almost reach the ground. He was not ridden much, so he was a little rusty. He was the only horse I was okay with loping on. A lope is faster than a trot and resembles a canter or gallop, but it is not as fast as a gallop. That little Haflinger would go running across the arena with me on him, and his short, coarse black and white mane would stand straight up in the air. I got a kick out of that funny little guy. I knew that if I got scared riding him, I could pretty much just stand up. I am sure I looked ridiculous. The more I laughed, the more this guy ran around. He was such a character.

· · · ● · ● · ● · · ·

On one occasion, a few other girls I had met there invited me to join them and participate in a team penning event. Team penning consists of a group of three people on horseback at one end of an arena, and thirty calves at the other end. Three calves wear the number zero, three wear the number one, three wear the number two, and so on, up to nine. There is a smaller round pen with an open gate in the middle of the arena. Once the three people on horseback walk over the center line, an announcer gives them a number between zero and nine. If that number is two, the riders need to work as a team to get all three of the designated number two calves into the round pen. They are given ninety seconds to do this. If a calf escapes the round pen or if a calf goes into the pen that does not have the designated number on it, you are disqualified. Before being invited to this event, I had never heard of team penning. I called Lucas, who was in Idaho, to run the idea by him. He encouraged me to give it a try.

Later that afternoon, we trailered our horses to the ranch hosting the event. None of our horses had ever been around calves before. The first thing we had to do was take them into the arena and warm them up while letting them get near the calves, which were on the other side of the fence in a holding pen.

I had decided to bring Comet, a seven-year-old, green-broke, leopard-spotted appaloosa, who I had started to become very attached to. The fact that he was young and had not had much training and I was relatively new to riding never seemed like a good idea to Lucas, who felt like I should be on a more experienced horse so I could learn things. Despite his concerns, Comet had a very sound mind, and he and I seemed to click well together. I felt safe with him. I knew he would never hurt me. In fact, the only thing that ever seemed to bother him was butterflies. Who knows how or why that fear started. In his head, butterflies were the scariest things on the planet. They were always enough of a threat to him, to totally distract him from whatever he had been doing and put him into total self-preservation mode, oblivious to the world around him. He would do a lot of bobbing and weaving with his head while jigging around trying to get away from them.

As we entered the arena for warm-ups, Comet seemed calm, unlike several of the other horses who were all sweaty and high-strung and obviously very anxious. I was proud of him. I walked him over to the calves. He went nose to nose with a few through the fence but otherwise seemed unfazed by them. Wow. I hadn't expected him to be so good with all of these new things but couldn't have been happier. Maybe team penning would be his thing. Every horse had certain areas they excelled at or preferred. We trotted around the ring with some of the other horses. Comet and I were warmed up and ready.

We lined up with the rest of the riders outside the arena and waited for our number to be called. Each of us had paid twenty dollars for four runs and was given a number. Our numbers were put into a bucket, and then we were randomly paired up with other riders. About half of the riders that night had never done this before, which took a lot of pressure off. There were about three times as many spectators as riders, sitting on blankets on the hill surrounding the arena. All of us riders were lined up around the top of that hill among intermittently placed, overflowing trash cans.

On our first run, Comet and I were teamed with one of the girls we came with, who had also never done this, and an older gentleman who seemed to have loads of experience. He liked to continuously tell us where to go and what to do, which was helpful and a little bit annoying. This was the first time our horses were actually in the arena with the calves. Up until now, the calves had been on the other side of the fence. This made a big difference to Comet, who seemed to be saying, "Whoa, what is going on here?" He was not so sure about this. However, once he realized he could chase these things, he thought that was great fun. Then it was hard to keep him focused on just one at a time. He was like a little boy with severe ADD, and

I couldn't keep control. I'd get him focused on one calf and the one next to him would move. Now we had to go get that one. Oh no, three moved over here, we need to go there now. All I could do was laugh. Comet seemed to be having so much fun. I don't think we got any calves in the round pen on that run.

The second run was a little better. I was paired with two other women I knew. One was an exceptionally good rider, and her horse was super high-strung at that moment. I believe she wanted to win this thing since she appeared so serious. Comet was a little more used to the calves by now. The three of us decided that Allie, our good rider, would sort the specific calves out of the group since Comet couldn't seem to focus, and I would drive them to the pen, hopefully allowing Comet to focus on one calf at a time. Erin, the other girl, would man the gate. She just had to keep the calves in the pen and make sure none of the others entered.

Allie separated the first calf from the herd of thirty very quickly, and I managed to walk him into the pen. I was beginning to get the hang of this. By the time I turned around, Allie had the second calf separated and was struggling a little with this guy; he was pretty quick and kept getting back with the herd. I went over to help, and we kept working at it. We eventually got the second calf in. The whole time, Allie was yelling, "Ya, ya, ya" and "Yip, yip," like she was on some sort of a cattle drive. Maybe that would help. So, on that third calf, I started yelling, "Ya, ya," like I was on the set of some old Western movie. I felt so ridiculous that I couldn't help myself; I busted out laughing. I was laughing so hard, in between every "Ya, ya" I was having a hard time breathing. I even had Allie cracking a smile.

At this point, the calves were all over the ring instead of bunched up together, and we were out of time. Since we had gotten two calves in the pen, we scored a two for that run. I felt okay with how well we were doing, especially since I had never heard of team penning three days before. In addition, I was having the most fun I had ever had on horseback.

On the third run, I was paired with two older gentlemen, who gave off a vibe as if they'd been doing this for most of their lives. I was sure they weren't happy about being paired with me. They were serious and, I could tell, super competitive. They decided to have me cover the gate, while they did the sorting. That was fine with me. I was game for whatever gave us the best chances. I could also be competitive. I would give it my all. There would be no ya ya's from me on this run. It was time to get serious.

As we entered the ring, we were given the number eight. I hurried to my position at the gate and these two guys got to work. Their skills at this were the best I had seen all night. The first calf was cut from the herd within about two seconds and was on his way into the pen. One down. By the time the first calf walked into the pen, the second one was on his way. Two down. These two guys were working as if they were one consistent fluid movement. They were each taking turns running the calves in. Everything was moving so fast, and I was starting to get excited with how well we were doing. The third calf took a little more finesse. That little guy was much shiftier than the first two. It took a little more time and both of those guys, one on each side of that calf, to bring him to the pen. Right before they got him to run into the pen, one of the other ones got out. Damn! That was my fault. The two I had had in the pen had been getting a little riled up. One of them, in particular, really wanted out and I was struggling to block him from getting through that open gate. It was getting dark and the overhead lights had just come on. Comet was struggling with who to pay attention to, the calves in the pen, or the one running toward the pen. I was trying to watch both at the same time and probably sending Comet mixed messages about which way to turn. We disqualified.

"Sorry guys," I said, as we walked out of the arena.

They were very gracious and encouraging. They tried to reassure me I would get it right next time.

As I was waiting for my next run and watching all of the other folks do the penning, a young guy, in his mid-twenties or so, was getting ready to enter the ring with two other riders. His horse, who was hands down the most high-strung, out-of-control horse at this entire event, so much so that we all stayed as far away from him as we could, decided he didn't like doing this after all. That horse took off at a dead sprint, around the back side of the arena, clear across the adjacent hayfield, over a hill on the adjoining property, and out of sight. To have a horse take off like that with me on it would have been my worst nightmare. I wondered why anybody in their right mind would even bring a horse like that to an event like this. Somebody could get seriously hurt. However, no one seemed very phased by this. The announcer simply called the next person who joined in on that run as if nothing happened. Team penning continued, never missing a beat.

By the time my number was called for the fourth run, I was starting to feel a little confident and thought I may have found my new passion in life. This was so much fun. On this run, I was paired with an older gray-haired lady, who looked every day of seventy, and one of the same guys I had been paired with on my last run. He suggested I cover the gate again since I hadn't done too badly before. I think he wanted me to try it again, and I was happy with that arrangement.

We entered the ring, were given our number, and started our run. The older lady with us was pretty good, almost as good as the other guy I had been paired with before. We got the first calf in pretty quickly—just as that runaway horse and rider came galloping back across the adjacent field, around the back of the arena, and crashed through the closed gate leading into the arena. The rider was desperately trying to get this horse under control. He had brief moments when we thought he was gaining control and then he would lose it again. He seemed to be using all his strength to pull back on the reins and stop that horse. I again wondered why this guy had a horse like that. Does he have a death wish, or is he just a cocky showboat cowboy?

That horse started rearing up and quickly moved backward. He ended up barreling sideways into the middle of the herd of twenty-eight calves, which resulted in complete calf chaos! Those calves started running in every direction, trying to get away from that crazy horse. Five more calves came running into the round pen. Comet started to come unglued and decided the only safe place was in the small round pen, behind the calves who were already in there. As he moved swiftly into the round pen, I instinctively reached out and managed to pull the gate most of the way closed behind me. I lost my grip as Comet scooted around those calves as quickly as he could. The elderly lady who was penning with us lost her seat and fell off her horse as he reared up trying to protect himself. Several young guys who had been watching from outside the arena jumped the fence and managed to get her out of the way of all of the stampeding animals. The other gentlemen I was paired up with eventually managed to grab ahold of that wild horse's reins, get a lead line on him, and subdue him enough to get him out of the arena and into a secure holding pen.

Before meeting Lucas, the last team sport I played was doubles tennis, and that wasn't anywhere near as exciting as this.

Over the loudspeaker, the host of this event announced we would be taking a fifteen-minute break while they switched out the calves for a new group, having thoroughly exhausted the first one. Most of the horses standing outside of the arena were amped up by this point. We needed that time to calm everyone down. Good grief! This was turning out to be a night to remember.

I took Comet back to the top of the hill and stood side by side with the other riders on their horses while attempting to settle him down so we could watch the rest of the runs that evening. We had finished all our runs. Despite what had just happened, I was enjoying team penning. Comet was doing well. I just needed to get him to focus a little better. And, I was still laughing the entire evening.

There was an overflowing trash can immediately in front of us with a group of high school girls on a blanket on the hill just in front of that. From hearing bits of their conversations, I could tell they were there watching a few of the younger male participants. They were all dressed in cowgirl outfits with full make-up, and their hair was done perfectly like they were competing in a Rodeo Queen contest. It was cute, and I briefly thought about how different my teenage years had been. Comet seemed fascinated with the contents of the trash can, and I had to keep backing him up from it. He was always so curious about everything around him. After a few minutes, he seemed to be calming down and started to stand quietly. He was such a good boy.

Allie and her horse were standing beside us, and we started talking, recapping the entire evening. I must have missed the run where Erin's reins broke and she had to finish her run steering her horse without them. At that moment, Erin walked up behind us, leading her horse. I turned in my seat to say something to her just as Comet moved forward. As I was talking, Erin started pointing in front of me, with her eyes huge. I turned back around just in time to catch Comet pick the side of that trash can up with his mouth and push it over, dumping the entire contents of empty and partially full soda cans, leftover nachos with cheese sauce, hotdogs with ketchup, tons of used napkins, dog poop someone had picked up, flies, and God knows what else all over those teenage girls, sitting quietly on the blanket in front of it. The minute it tipped over, Comet immediately took two steps back and stood quietly, as if saying, "I didn't do that." He was like a bored little kid, willing to do anything for attention.

"Oh my God!!! Oh no! I am so, so sorry," I repeated. At the same time, I found myself wanting to laugh. Those poor girls! Oh, but it was so funny. I was trying so hard not to laugh in front of them.

Those girls looked back at us with the most surprised looks of shock and disbelief I have ever seen. I wasn't sure if I should take Comet back to the trailer and never show my face here again or get off my horse and help them clean up.

I looked over at Allie who was biting her lip. She turned completely around on her horse so she wouldn't bust out laughing in front of them. I jumped off Comet and gave Allie his rein while I attempted to help clean up the trash and convince the girls this was an accident. They were so shocked; they didn't know what to say. I have now completely ruined their evening, and all they kept saying was "It's okay," and looking at each other while we all picked up trash and put it back in the can. They spent what little time was left of that evening trying to get all of the various drinks, kinds of ketchup, mustard, cheese sauce, dog poop, and whatever else had been in that trash can off of their clothing.

I think I laughed more on the way home from that event that night than I ever had in my life. I laughed at everything from the trash dump to yelling, "Ya, ya, yip, yip, yip" in the arena, to the wild horse crashing our run, resulting in an "every calf and person for themselves" type of chaos. At that moment, even Grandma falling off her horse seemed funny. I was also convinced that Comet had a sense of humor. There was no doubt in my mind, and I loved that about him.

Later that night, as I was crawling into bed still chuckling, I realized how much laughing hard like that was so good for my soul. I had been missing that in my life before Lucas.

· · • • • • • • · ·

I learned so much riding all those different horses and had so much fun, especially with Comet. I went down there to ride and play with the horses every chance I had. The only time I wasn't allowed to ride in the arena was when it had a fair amount of standing water in it. I figured it was too slippery for the horses but never really asked the reason why. However, I was still not comfortable going any faster than a trot, much to my husband's frustration. On the rare occasions when he would go riding with me, he would periodically threaten to come up behind me and smack my horse on the butt, making him lope. I am sure I threatened him with something worse if he ever tried that because he never did. I knew he was frustrated with my stalled progress. It had been a year since Mabel took off with me, and I just did not know how to overcome my fear of loping.

Lucas finally suggested I try taking lessons somewhere else. I was stuck trotting and no matter what anybody else said or did, I was not ready to lope. I could not seem to shake that "what if." At the same time, I was worried that I would never live up to Lucas's expectations or be able to keep up with him on horseback. I wanted to—so bad.

· · • • • • • • · ·

I finally started taking lessons from a guy in Winchester who seemed to know exactly how much to push me and when to back off. He sensed that what I needed was to get my mind off the "what if," and just do it. He was right. He came up with little drills, like carrying a golf ball on a spoon, while I walked around the ring and then trot with it. I was so focused on keeping that ball on the spoon, that when he told me to ask the horse for a lope, I did it. Afterward, I realized that it was not so bad. We did many drills like that one.

One day, I showed up for a lesson, got my horse out of the barn, and rode her down to the arena, where I always met Matt, my instructor. It had rained hard the night before and half of the sand and bluestone arena was underwater.

"Uh oh. I guess we are not doing our lesson in the arena today, huh," I remarked.

"Why not?"

"Because it is mostly underwater?" I said, questioning the obvious here.

"Well, horses have been running through water for thousands of years. This is no different. Get on in here."

Matt sensed my fearfulness of the water situation and was now planning on using it as some sort of lesson. I just knew it. I had never run a horse through water, only walked through creeks—up until now. I wondered what the odds were of my horse slipping and falling while running through it.

There was no walking through this water first. No time to think too much about it. Matt asked me to go right into a lope around the ring. I started on the dry side, and when I got to the wet side, I instinctively tried to cut in front of the water and stay dry.

"What are you doing?" He hollered. "Do it again and I want you to go right through that water."

Well, crap. Here we go. Don't think about it—just do it. This time we managed to only go through the edge of the water. It was shallower there. *At least I did it. Maybe now we can do something else?*

"Again. This time, go all the way through the water," Matt insisted.

With that, Matt walked over and blocked my horse from doing anything but going through the deepest part. And when I started to unconsciously slow my horse down while going through it, he was right there with a lunge whip, anticipating that I would do exactly that.

"That's it. Now keep her going and do it again. Keep your leg on her and do not slow down."

This time, Matt retreated to the middle of the arena and I was on my own. I did it. I did it three more times, before stopping. I felt so proud of myself. To my surprise, that was really fun. We switched directions and loped the other way. I realized there was a time and a place to put my trust in my horse. This was one of those times. Once I did, everything was fine.

With Matt, I progressed quickly and was loping not only in the arena but also in the woods and through creeks with him. I will never forget the day Mabel scared the pants off me, but I was chipping away at my fear, bit by bit, and I could not wait to get my own horse someday. Was that going to happen? I sure hoped so.

Before any of that could happen, we needed to figure out where we were going to live once both of my boys were off to college.

4

Finding Our Place

We planned to spend the month of September driving across the country, through South Dakota, Montana, Idaho, Utah, all over Colorado, and a little piece of New Mexico, scouting out areas that we may eventually want to retire to. The only one of those states I had been to was Utah because that is where my oldest son was now in college. We were newly married, and just before leaving for this trip, I remember thinking that spending all this time with anyone for a month, never mind in Lucas's small Prius, was going to be challenging by itself. It would either make us better together or ruin us.

Having spent my entire career in corporate sales of one sort or another and countless hours driving DC's Capital Beltway, mostly in stop-and-go traffic, I was burned out. Lucas had spent his entire adult life in Virginia and raised his family in nearby Loudon County. He had been able to retire at age forty-four, after growing a hugely successful gym business in Fairfax County. We were both beyond done with the horrendous traffic in the area and struggled with the high humidity and heat in the summers. Lucas had also managed a large cattle ranch in Hume immediately after graduating from Rutgers University, and more recently had his own cattle ranch in Purcellville. We had been discussing the possibility of doing something like that again out west.

I was pleasantly surprised by how much fun this trip was, even though we did have a few hiccups. We had no agenda. Every night, after checking into a hotel, usually Hampton Inns because I have a thing about raunchy motels, we would look at a map, decide where we would like to get to the next day, and then consult the AAA books to find out what there was to see along the way. Once I realized I didn't have to stress about finding a vacancy in a hotel, there always was one, I felt incredibly liberated and free.

We didn't get out of busier traffic until we got to Davenport, Iowa. After that, it started to feel more like rural America. From there, we went north to Sioux Falls and drove west across South Dakota, going through the Badlands, the Black Hills, and Sturgis. We stopped in Deadwood and did the popular tourist attractions, including visiting the saloon where Wild Bill Hickok was shot and Boot Hill Cemetery, where Calamity Jane is buried. We saw Mt. Rushmore, stopped in the visitor center, and paid for the tour of the Crazy Horse monument, which will take about another one hundred years to finish constructing. We even made a quick stop at Wall Drug after seeing more billboards advertising it than billboards advertising South of the Border in the Carolinas. I have always loved American history, and it was everywhere out here. In addition, I had watched close to every Western movie and was thoroughly enjoying this trip.

Once we left South Dakota and started across Montana, we stopped at more obscure places. For instance, one Saturday morning, we pulled off the highway and into the parking lot of a local high school rodeo competition. I couldn't believe high school kids were bull and bareback bronc riding. I had been okay with my kids playing football and lacrosse, but I am not sure I would have signed off on them riding bulls in their teens.

We stopped in an old west town called Virginia City where people were dressed in period costumes. It reminded me of a much smaller-scale Williamsburg attraction. We saw pronghorn antelope and drove through the National Bison Range. We even stopped at a local ranch we had seen advertised for several miles. Everything there, including the house and barn, was staged just like it had been in the late 1800s. There were draft horses for pulling plows and wagons.

They even had what they referred to as cowboy coffee outside next to a covered wagon. I didn't try that, but Lucas did. Lucas likes his coffee black and way stronger than anyone I know, and even he said that the coffee was too strong.

We drove across Montana and stopped near Dillon. While we were enjoying this trip, as far as finding a place to move to, I was disappointed. I had high hopes for us finding our place in Montana and settling down on a small cattle ranch. I expected it to be prettier. There was plenty of big sky but very few trees. Lucas suggested we take a few days and drive up to Glacier National Park. That sounded good to me.

Still being early September, we were lucky enough to find a vacancy at an adorable B&B right outside of the park and spent three days there exploring Glacier. We drove the Going-to-the-Sun Road through the park, each way, stopping to hike on several different trails, each one more gorgeous than the previous one. We saw mountain goats that walked right up to us, big horn sheep, stunning waterfalls, and lakes with the clearest blue water I have ever seen. The water was so pretty that at one point, we felt compelled to take off our hiking boots to put our feet in the icy water. We had picnics on rocks next to waterfalls. I must have taken a thousand photos. If they had let me build a house in the middle of Glacier, I don't think I ever would have left. In my opinion, it is the most beautiful place in this country. This entire northwest corner of Montana was stunning and very different from the rest of Montana.

We planned to leave there, drive to north Idaho, and then south to Grangeville, Idaho. Lucas had this idea that we were going to end up in Grangeville because he had heard so many great things about it.

• • • • • • • • • •

On our last morning at the B&B, during breakfast, a series of events started to unfold that would have even the most skeptical people believing in pure providence. We overheard an older couple at the table next to us talking about going home to Bonners Ferry. Lucas, never wanting to miss an opportunity, went over and started a conversation with them about what we were doing on our trip and how we were heading to Bonners Ferry, Idaho later that day. They were very gracious and gave us a few ideas on where to look. They said they were on their second marriage and had done the same thing we were doing, only about ten years ago. They had been in Bonners Ferry ever since and loved it. We thanked them and were on our way.

About three hours later, we were stopped in traffic due to some road construction near the Idaho border for what seemed to be an hour, although I am sure it wasn't quite that long. We didn't mind since it was simply beautiful in that part of Montana. We could not have asked for a prettier, sunny September day. The sky is so much bluer there than on the East Coast. Both sides of the road were lined with different types of pine trees, their vivid green complimenting the blue sky. We witnessed no road rage or people flipping each other off. Everyone seemed perfectly content to sit and enjoy the scenery—a far cry from the Capital Beltway. Several people in front of us had even gotten out of their cars and were smiling and talking with each other. What a welcome change this was.

At some point, someone knocked on our car window. It was the lady from the table next to us at the B&B. They just happened to be sitting right behind us in traffic. After a few minutes of talking to them on the side of the road, the gentleman looked at his wife and asked her, "Are you thinking what I am thinking?"

"Yes," she quickly replied.

He then proceeded to tell us about a piece of property across the road from their place that was for sale and he just happened to be the listing real estate agent. He reiterated that that was not why he was telling us about it but that it sounded like what we were looking for and they'd love to have us as neighbors, which was very nice of them. We thanked them and told them we weren't quite ready to buy yet. They understood and he gave us his card in case we changed our minds.

Traffic finally started moving and as we were approaching Bonners Ferry a little while later, we started thinking, *What could it hurt to look at that property?* So, we called the agent. At this point, he apologized and said he had just made dinner plans, but he would be happy to show it to us in the morning. We thanked him again and told him we were going to be south of Bonners Ferry by then and not to bother with it. I think he felt bad, so just before hanging up, he gave us the names of three restaurant recommendations in Sandpoint, which is where we were planning on stopping for the night.

Another hour or so later, we were driving over the long bridge in Sandpoint, and it was getting close to 5:00. This was a gorgeous area where Lake Pend Oreille, a forty-three-mile lake surrounded by pine trees and mountains, stood. The water was a dark blue color and there were several boats sprinkled intermittently in it. There was even a ski resort, Schweitzer, that we could easily see from the lake. There were several white sand beaches we could see from the bridge and a smattering of nice-looking homes randomly placed on the sides of the mountains around the lake—most had staircases going down to private docks. What else could you want? This place looked perfect. There was something for every season. I had not realized there were places in this country this pretty. I was seriously in awe of it.

I asked Lucas, "Do you have any interest in trying out one of those restaurants that the agent suggested?"

"Actually, I am kind of tired. Do you mind if we just pick up a pizza or something and go and eat in the hotel room?"

"I don't mind at all. But, one of the restaurants he suggested is right there in front of us on the water, and it looks nice. This place is stunning."

"OK," he said. "If you want to try it, I guess we can do that."

As we were walking into the lobby, I noticed they weren't busy yet. That's always a good thing. There was only one other couple in the lobby in front of us. As we got closer to them, I could not believe my eyes. It was that same couple. They were meeting some friends there. At this point, Lucas and I looked at each other and said, "OK. I think we must go look at that property in the morning." It seemed the universe was trying to tell us something.

The next morning, we drove the hour back up to Bonners Ferry and met the agent at the property. It was one hundred forty acres of secluded bare land with unbelievable views of the mountains all the way around. It was partially open field, partially wooded, and surrounded on three sides by state and forest service land. It was extremely remote. We could even see the slopes at Schweitzer Ski Resort in the distance.

As we were driving up the terribly steep and somewhat treacherous driveway that would have to be redone if we purchased this place, there were these very large strange-looking birds running alongside the car. I had never seen anything like them before. They looked a little prehistoric to me. Once I asked, I found out they were wild turkeys. That was something I did not see in the suburbs of Washington, DC. When we got to the top of the driveway, we were in an open flat field; I was absolutely mesmerized by the views. The people selling it lived back in Maryland and just wanted to be rid of it. I could not imagine why. This property seemed like one in a million. The state land that ran along the backside of this field was a mountain with a bunch of horseback riding trails that went up and over it. The agent and his wife also rode horses and told us that we could almost ride to Montana without crossing a road from there. But, again, Lucas and I were not ready to buy. After all, I had not even seen Colorado yet and had high hopes for the Durango area simply from what I had read about it. We thanked him and told him that it was a beautiful piece of property, but we had to think it over.

We left and continued south on Highway 95 in Idaho toward Grangeville; Lucas was so eager to see it. These were the days before every vehicle had a GPS, and the ones you plugged into the cigarette lighters were not always accurate, so I was the navigator with a road map on my lap. Idaho, so far, has been nothing short of absolutely stunning. We were both very optimistic about it. Lucas had been to Idaho one time previously and said there was only one area in all of Idaho that we could skip because he thought it was one of the ugliest places he had ever seen. That was Salmon.

We drove south and around Lake Coeur d' Alene. It was pretty, but nothing like Lake Pend Oreille in Sandpoint. Several hours later, somewhere between St. Maries and Moscow, Lucas reminded me, "Make sure we don't miss the turn-off to Grangeville."

"I got it," I replied.

We stopped for lunch in Moscow and visited the Appaloosa Heritage Museum since it was right off the highway. I could not get over how beautiful this area was. The road wound through these mountains. Idaho's Highway 95 was nothing like Interstate 95 on the East Coast. Here, it was mostly two lanes. At times, the scenery left me awestruck. We drove through Orofino, Riggins, and New Meadows. If possible, things were just getting prettier. I must have lost track of time because a short while later, a sign popped up for McCall, Idaho.

Lucas calmly asked, "Abby, how far to the turn-off to Grangeville?"

I felt a slight panic go through me as I consulted the map.

"Oops! That was about an hour ago. Sorry."

"Abby!"

"I am sorry. Everything is just so pretty."

Lucas took that well and he let it go, as we continued toward Challis. That was going to be our stop for the night. I usually took care of booking our hotels. However, since there were no Hampton Inns in the area, Lucas offered to take care of it for tonight.

After spending several hours winding through back mountain roads as we cut across Idaho, we finally arrived in Challis. I was surprised to see how small it was—it was tiny, maybe six buildings total. We pulled into our hotel, and it looked pretty darn sketchy. It was a square cinderblock building with very few windows. It more closely resembled a prison, of sorts. I looked at Lucas funny. As if reading my mind, he said, "Hey, there are only two hotels here, and this was the more expensive one."

"How much was it?"

"Fifty dollars a night."

Oh my gosh! He knows I have a huge issue with raunchy hotels. What is he thinking? This is never going to work.

As we walked into the lobby, there was no formal front desk or a coffee station. There was an 8-foot folding table, probably from Costco, with an old white stained Mr. Coffee machine on it. It was half full, and I was sure it had been sitting there since morning. This doubled as the front desk and coffee station. There were no freshly baked cookies or continental breakfasts served here. To top it off, the young girl who was working there had pink hair, a large nose ring, and looked like she was about seventeen years old.

Despite all of that, we checked in and went to our room, which was in the basement. Inside the room was a double bed with a bedspread that looked like it was straight out of the 1970s with large green and yellow flowers. There was one folding metal chair by the window and a very old thirteen-inch, black and white TV mounted to the wall with a remote control next to the bed. I was surprised it even had a remote. The walls were unpainted cinderblocks. I hadn't even looked at the bathroom. Quite frankly, I was afraid to. The whole place had a musty smell that I associated with my grandmother's basement when I was a kid, which was full of spiders and other creepy crawly things. *There is no way I am staying here. I would rather sleep in the car. Can Lucas really be serious?*

Sensing my discomfort, Lucas walked over to me and put his arms around me.

"Honey, we have been driving for eight hours already today, and my back is killing me. Can we just make this do for one night? It won't kill us."

"OK," I hesitantly replied, wanting to work with him on this but not sure I could.

All I wanted to do was get back in the car and drive away from there. *As much as I want to do this for Lucas, this may be too much for me to handle.* I sat in the metal folding chair, contemplating a way out of this, while he sat on the bed, which squeaked loudly when he did. He turned the TV on, and after a minute or so, said, "Come and sit next to me."

"OK," I sheepishly replied.

I walked over and immediately picked up a long hair that was on top of the bed.

"Honey, it's probably just from the girl making the bed."

"Ok," I said, but since it was not pink, I knew better.

I then pulled the bedspread and top sheet back a little and we watched a bug about the size of a stink bug, walk across the sheets. I did not have to say another word. Thank God.

"OK," Lucas said. "Get your stuff; this will not work."

We checked out and were on our way. We had planned to drive to Idaho Falls the next day before stopping over in Salt Lake City the following day to see my son, Billy. There was nothing between here and there. There was so much wilderness in Idaho. This ride was going to take another five or so hours, and it was already 6 p.m. Once again, I was navigating. Lucas was not happy, mostly because his back was killing him from driving all day. I offered to drive, but he insisted, saying I made him car sick by pumping the gas. I do not think I do that, but he does. We had driven 2,600 miles, and he had not let me drive once, convinced that is why my dog got car sick.

We arrived at the next intersection.

"Which way, Abby?" Lucas asked a little curtly.

"Left."

As we continued, Lucas was flying on the back roads. I know he just wanted to get to our Hampton Inn in Idaho Falls and out of the car as soon as possible. We drove through a pretty good thunderstorm and saw a magnificent rainbow afterward. I had no idea there was so much beauty in Idaho. After three hours we had not passed a town, or even a gas station. Then suddenly, a sign popped up that said WELCOME TO SALMON. Oh no! Salmon was north of Challis and Idaho Falls was south. *Crap! I must have screwed up again.* Lucas took one deep breath and seemed to be holding his breath after that. He had not said a word in the five minutes since we saw that sign. We pulled into a Burger King. Still not saying anything, we walked inside, used the bathrooms, and I got something to eat. Lucas said he was not hungry and went out to the car. As I walked back out to the car, he was standing on the passenger side. As he threw me the car keys, he said, "You're driving."

"OK," I said, not knowing how to react in this instance.

In the two years that I had been with Lucas, we had never fought. This had the makings of our first big fight, and it was my fault. I got into the car and noticed that he had a freshly opened bottle of red wine on his lap.

"Are we drinking?" I asked.

"Yep."

"From the bottle?"

"Yep."

"OK then. I am sorry."

He just nodded his head.

A little over seven hours later, we pulled into the Hampton Inn in Idaho Falls. It was now the wee hours of the morning, and Lucas was no longer upset, having drank that entire bottle of wine by himself. We checked in and grabbed a few hours of sleep before we had to check out. A Hampton Inn bed had never felt better. I was so glad we hadn't had a big fight. I truly felt bad for screwing up but extremely relieved that we were out of that cheap hotel in Challis.

• • • • ● • ● • • •

Several days later, we kept going back and talking about how much we liked that property in Bonners Ferry. Lucas came up with a plan. He suggested we make an offer—a lowball, cash offer. We'd tell them we are not going to negotiate. It will be a one-time offer. That is what we did. We gave them seventy-two hours to decide whether to accept it. The agent called us back almost immediately and said he didn't think the sellers were going to accept the offer but that they were going to sleep on it.

We continued on our trip and drove all through western Colorado. Durango was too crowded and seemed like a college town to me—not exactly what we wanted. I did love some of the areas in Colorado, particularly Steamboat Springs and Ouray, but felt they were a little on the pricey side. We drove through Taos, New Mexico. Interesting place. It was very artsy and whimsical, which was definitely not my vibe. Just outside of Taos, in what looked like a desert, were a whole smattering of large, expensive-looking houses that appeared as if they belonged in Dr. Suess's Whoville. They were the strangest-looking houses I have ever seen. I was quietly keeping my fingers crossed about that property in Bonners Ferry.

A few days later, we were getting close to home. We were somewhere in Kentucky and approaching seventy hours since we made that offer, when suddenly Lucas's phone rang. What do you know, they accepted our offer. *Hold on a minute. They what?* As much as I had liked that property, I was now a jumble of mixed feelings. The most powerful feeling I had was fear. I was scared to death of what this meant. The first thing out of my mouth was not

"Yay," or "Oh, that is so awesome," but, "Holy shit! What have we done?"

There didn't seem to be any turning back from that point. I was excited somewhere inside and scared to death of what this meant—moving across the country. This dream was becoming a reality, and yet, I was about to have an anxiety attack. We were committed now. *Oh my gosh, what if I change my mind?* I had lived my entire life between Baltimore and Washington, D.C. Everything and everyone I knew were there. We had just purchased one hundred forty acres of secluded bare land in northern Idaho about as far north as you could get without going into Canada. What had I been thinking?

Little did I know that the biggest adventure of our lives was just beginning!

5

Moving to Idaho

Lucas purchased our current house in Gainesville in 2011, right after we were married. Since Lucas's house had been in an entirely different county, and it was important to me to keep my boys in the same high school until they graduated, it made sense to Lucas. He was not a fan of renting.

Our plan had been to time our move to Idaho to happen right after my youngest son went off to college—sometime in August of 2015. Kevin was graduating from high school in May of 2015 and was planning on following his brother Billy, to the University of Utah that fall. At that time, all six of our kids would be living all over the country, with one living in Australia temporarily. We would love to be closer to our kids, but since they were so scattered, we felt it didn't matter where we went. By now, I was working as a real estate agent in Virginia and planned to get Kevin off to college in August and sell our house just before moving to Idaho.

Lucas went to Idaho during the summer of 2014, built a workshop with an apartment on either end, and came home in September. He left the following April to go back and start building the house, while he stayed in one of the apartments. He planned to have the house completed by the time I got there in late summer of 2015. I had never built a house before. Lucas let me pick the house plans and make any changes I thought were necessary while he built it. He texted me daily photos of the progress he was making. It was all super exciting, and I could not wait to see it in person.

Plans sometimes need to be altered. Kevin changed his plans to follow his brother to the University of Utah at the last minute, deciding instead to go to Virginia Tech and stay on the East Coast. Our house in Virginia sold much quicker than anticipated. After several tearful goodbyes to friends and family and an especially emotional one to Kevin since he was my youngest and now staying on the East Coast, I found myself driving across the country with my Goldendoodle, Grady, and my seventy-six-year-young dad to keep me company in mid-July.

It is about a four-day drive. As soon as we left, my emotions were such a mix of anxiety, panic attacks, and excitement. It is a wonder I didn't just crumble. I was full of sadness and trepidation about leaving everything and everyone I had ever known and excited about what this next chapter in my life would bring. At times, I even second-guessed my decision and wondered if I had lost my mind. In fact, within the previous thirty days, I had more than one person ask me if I was sure I knew what I was doing, adding to the growing doubt in my head. Going 2,400 miles away, where I only knew my husband, was super scary. However, I was starting over fresh after an ugly divorce. I did not want to look back, only forward. Someone once told me there is a reason that the windshield is bigger than the rearview mirror. That seemed appropriate now.

In addition, I couldn't help but wonder if I was really over the wounds of the infidelities and lies of my first marriage. Did the type of loyalty I wanted and, more importantly, needed in a partnership really exist? I wanted the type of love and commitment that can endure anything. I sometimes wondered if that only existed in fairy tales. I knew in my heart I could never settle for less. Yet, sometimes I wondered if my expectations were too high. Because of that, was I doomed to spend the rest of my life alone? Because of that, I knew I was guarded with my feelings.

In my teenage years, when confronted with an unpleasant break-up, I recalled my dad telling me not to wear my heart on my sleeve. I took that seriously and became more stoic with my emotions in future relationships. Lucas completely disagreed with this philosophy. He felt it was better to be vulnerable and put oneself out there. He preferred the "nothing ventured, nothing gained" attitude.

On this drive, I felt so fortunate and grateful to be able to spend uninterrupted time with my dad. We had never spent much time together, just us. What a bonus this was. We talked about everything and sang to music. I had never known my dad to sing before, and that was fun. Finding dog-friendly hotels wasn't as difficult as I expected either. We took a few side trips. I wanted my dad to see the Badlands, the Blackhills, and Deadwood, which he especially loved.

My dad, Grady, and I walked all over Deadwood, talking about what it must have been like when it was first established. We both shared the same fondness for the history of the American West.

When leaving South Dakota, we traveled through an Indian reservation in the northeast corner of Wyoming. Lucas and I had not gone that way, so I thought we'd try something different. There was no cell service for about three hours and nothing to see—not even a gas station. After the first two hours, my dad said, "I am really glad I came with you."

I thanked him and reminded him I did have AAA if I needed to call them. To which he replied, "And where do you think they are going to come from?"

"Good point, Dad."

We chuckled a little.

Over the next two days, we made one more side trip to Glacier National Park. My dad seemed to enjoy that side trip the most. On our last night, before arriving in Bonners Ferry, we stayed at a beautiful golf resort in Whitefish, Montana, which was right up my dad's alley. Golf had been his passion for most of his life. We had a delicious late dinner overlooking the course while golfers were still finishing up at 9:00 in the evening. It didn't get dark until almost 10:00 here. I will forever remember this trip. Being able to spend that time with my dad made it so special. What a memory we made. I wished we had done more of this type of stuff in my lifetime.

• • • • ● • ● • • •

Finally, we arrived in Bonners Ferry and at our property. The house was getting close to being finished. Lucas had been working tirelessly to get it done, but it was going to take two to three more weeks until it was ready for us to move in. In the meantime, we would stay in the eight-hundred-square-foot, one-bedroom apartment that Lucas built alongside his shop, which was at the bottom of the hill from the house.

I felt like I had been plucked from civilization and plopped down in the middle of the wilderness, which is not far from the truth. I had been told there were grizzlies, black bears, mountain lions, wolves, coyotes, moose, tons of elk and deer, and wild turkey here. We couldn't see or hear any neighbors from our place—just wildlife, and boy did we see that.

The first thing I noticed was that the days were much longer than I was used to since we were so much further north. It didn't get dark until almost 10 at night and the sun was up by 4 a.m. The summer weather was just perfect. No need for an air conditioner here. The days were mostly between seventy-five to eighty-two with no humidity and the nighttime temperatures were in the fifties. We just slept with the windows open, which came with a few issues at first.

I was so used to hearing cars and sirens all night long in Virginia, that this unusual quiet stillness made it hard for me to sleep for the first few nights. Those first nights were full of intermittent strange animal noises that sounded, and probably were, very close. This resulted in me waking Lucas up multiple times a night to ask what those noises were. There were strange snorting sounds, wild turkey noises, and the first time I heard an elk bugle, Lucas and I about knocked each other over trying to get to the window. It was the middle of the night with a full moon that lit up our entire back field of seventy acres. There was an entire herd of thirty or so elk in that field with a huge bull elk bugling right outside of our window. He was maybe fifteen feet from us. What a majestic sight. He was as big as a horse with a humongous rack on his head. If it was as heavy as it looked, I don't know how he held his head up. I stood staring at him, completely mesmerized for several minutes, afraid to even breathe for fear I would scare him away. I felt so privileged to have seen this sight. When he started to walk off, I felt disappointed. By now, Lucas was back in bed, telling me that I had to stop waking him up so many times every night because no one was getting any sleep.

The very next night, in the middle of the night again, I woke to what sounded like someone repeatedly shooting a gun in our backyard. I nudged Lucas, shocked that he was able to sleep through it, and told him, "Someone is shooting an automatic gun in our field."

He assured me, "No one is shooting a gun in our field. The sound just carries through these canyons."

It kept happening.

"Lucas, I'm telling you they are close. You have to do something."

"Abby, what do you want me to do? I am not going out there in the woods in the dark with someone shooting."

I said, "Call the police."

"They're not coming," replied Lucas. "This is north Idaho. People shoot guns here. It's okay. I am sure they are not as close as you think."

· · · ● · ● · · ·

The next morning, while Lucas was working on the house with the contractors, I decided I would put on shorts, sit outside with Grady, and maybe get a little sun. I hadn't gotten much sleep the night before due to the shooting, so I thought I might even take a nap. After about fifteen minutes, Grady came over and stood up against me. Odd, but okay. He wouldn't normally do that. Next, he started barking under his breath, looking into the woods about ten feet from us. That started to make the hairs on the back of my neck stand up.

"OK, let's go in," I said, as I grabbed his leash, slightly frustrated that the morning was not going according to plan.

Not three seconds later, as I was closing the apartment door and looking out the window, a momma black bear and two young cubs, a cinnamon one and a black one, came out of the woods, walked right next to my chair, across the yard, and down the driveway. *Holy Cow! What just happened?* I lost my breath for a second. At the same time, I couldn't help but think, *How cool was that?* They were literally ten feet from me. It became apparent to me that we were now in their backyard.

Lucas and I would sit on the front porch in the evenings until it cooled off a little inside. There was a resident turkey with thirteen chicks that was always hanging around. She would hide in the deep grass in the field, not too far from where we were sitting. Once in a while, we would see her head pop up as if to see if we were still there. It became like a game to us, wondering where she was going to pop up next. On rare occasions, she would cross the driveway in front of us with all thirteen chicks following. We even named her "Butterball and her thirteen babies."

What a beautiful and wonderfully unexpected surprise, how much joy one can discover spending time in nature. This was something I had never considered before moving here. The wildlife here is spectacular.

Not long after that, we were able to move into our new house and order furniture. This was the first house I had ever built and designed. Lucas built it. He had built many of his own houses as well as others in the past, and he is exceptionally good at it. The fact that he let me run with pretty much whatever I wanted to do with the house really made me feel like a Queen. I loved that house and him even more for making our dreams come true.

Our house was on the top of a hill, in the middle of our fields. It had a walk-out basement with two guest rooms, a bathroom, and a large recreational area with a pool table. There was a covered patio with a built-in fire pit. Our bedroom, office, kitchen, dining room, and family room were on the main level, along with a huge covered front porch and back deck. Lucas had even built a nice porch swing for the front porch. We had a large laundry/mud room on the way into the garage. In addition, we could walk through the garage to access Lucas's woodshop, which was attached to the other side. His main shop was at the bottom of the hill. The entire house consisted of no more than 3,500 square feet. Yet, every time a neighbor would see it for the first time, they would always ask, "Why did you build such a big house?" For north Idaho, I suppose it seemed big.

One of the big challenges we faced was going to be getting grass to grow around the house. Lucas brought in truckloads of topsoil to put on top of all the sand that we had. That is all we had—sand as far down as you could dig. This property must have been part of a delta when all the glaciers were melting many, many years ago. He then spent hours putting grass seed down and watering it. In hindsight, we may have been better off putting in sand volleyball courts.

Within a few days of doing this, we woke up to a bunch of turkeys in the yard, eating the grass seed. Lucas was not having that. He went running outside in his underwear, since we have no neighbors anywhere around us, shooing those turkeys out of the yard. This went on for a couple of days. The turkeys were getting braver and braver and were no longer afraid of Lucas. Next, he went running outside with his shotgun and shot it up in the air to scare them off. That worked for a few days, but again, they became braver and returned. That did it. The next time they came into the yard, Lucas was ready and determined he was going to take care of this for good. He was now going to get his shotgun and pepper their little hinnies, with number eight skeet shot, assuring me he would "only sting them and teach them a lesson," as he put it. As he was inside loading his gun, I went out on the porch and desperately tried to shoo the turkeys into the woods. I believe I even said, "Are you guys crazy? He's getting the gun. Get out of here!"

Lucas must have been behind me when I said that. The next thing I heard was a loud bang, and suddenly, three turkeys went down and were wildly flailing their wings on the ground. With my mouth wide open, I turned around and gave Lucas a look as if he'd shot our family dog.

"Oops," was all he said.

"Well," I said, clearly upset, "you cannot leave them like that. You have to put them out of their misery."

I was mad at Lucas and upset that those poor animals were now writhing in pain. Lucas ran inside to get his pistol.

He went and stood over one of them and shot it. It was still flailing.

"Shoot it again," I said. "It is not dead." I was close to tears and so worried about them suffering unnecessarily.

"Oh honey, it's dead."

"No, it's not. It's still flapping around."

"Honey, it doesn't have a head."

"Oh God."

I guess there is some truth to the idea of a chicken, or turkey in this case, running around with its head chopped off.

He took care of the other two fairly quickly. He then looked at me and said, "Well, since we have them, what do you say we breast them and try cooking them up?"

"Sure," I said, as I turned to leave to run errands in town, wondering if I had the stomach for this life.

I could not wait to get away from this whole scene. *Will it make me a tough enough country girl, if I can cook and eat these turkey breasts?* I wondered.

After two days of brining those breasts and cooking them all day in the crockpot, they were not edible. They were as tough as nails, and the meat was all dark, not that there was much of it on our scrawny wild turkeys anyway. We were better off enjoying them from the porch.

We had also been enjoying large herds of elk in our back field several times every week. They sure were majestic, and we would sit on the back porch with a glass of wine in the evenings and watch them for hours. One night, we counted seventy-three elk, forty-three whitetail deer, six mule deer, and God only knows how many turkeys. They were all in our seventy-acre field at the same time. It was like our own wild kingdom.

Lucas asked me what I thought of getting an elk and trying it this year. "You mean killing it and eating it?"

"Yes."

"I don't know, Lucas. I love watching them from the porch, but if I saw it being killed, I don't think I could eat it. Maybe we should stick with beef."

The only wild game I had ever eaten was venison, and I didn't care much for its gamey flavor.

"Elk is supposed to be really good and leaner than beef. I told our neighbor, John, that he could hunt in our back field for an elk as long as he gives us half."

"What? You did that without talking to me first? Lucas, I don't want to be sitting out here watching them one night when John shoots one in front of us."

"I'll make sure he does it in the way back where you can't see it."

"Really?"

I was not happy about it, but was not sure how far to push this one. Maybe John would not have any luck with killing an elk, and it would not be an issue. I wished Lucas would slow down my acclimation to this lifestyle a bit and ease me into things like this.

Two months later, John called to say he had gotten an elk. I did not know how to feel about it. He was, apparently, super happy. A few days later, he delivered our half of the elk, already processed and wrapped, along with a vanilla latte for me. I sensed Lucas had informed him of my mixed emotions about killing an elk, and this was some sort of peace offering, which I accepted. He did make the best lattes.

Half of an elk is enough food to feed a family of four for a year. I could not believe how much meat there was. It turned out that I liked the taste of it. To me, it tasted like a good cut of beef, just leaner. It had to be healthier. I established that I can eat wild game, at least elk, as long as it comes to me all processed, cut up, and packaged. It was no different from buying it in the store. I, however, wanted no part of the killing.

Now that the house was almost finished and we were completely moved in, the next project would be a barn and fencing for the horses we were planning to get. I had never had my own horse and really could not wait for that. In the meantime, I needed to get familiar with my new town and was looking forward to meeting some of our neighbors.

6

The Neighbors

While Lucas had been busy finishing the house, I took that time to get to know our little town and meet some neighbors. So far, the only neighbors we knew were the couple we met in Glacier, Bud, our realtor, his wife, Lindsey, and John and Becky, who live just down the road. After mentioning to Lindsey that we planned to get horses once we built a barn and put fencing in, she suggested I may like Katey, another neighbor, who was really into riding and had a bunch of horses.

One morning on my way back from town, on a whim, I pulled into Katey's driveway and introduced myself. She was standing just outside of her barn with her two beautiful teenage daughters. Katey was a few years younger than me, and we instantly hit it off. After a few minutes, she asked if I could help her judge a horse show the next day.

"Sure," I said.

It was a small schooling horse show with mostly 4-H kids in it. The event went smoothly, and I met a few other people who were mostly 4-H moms. Everyone seemed super nice. After the show, I was talking to Katey in the parking lot and happened to mention that I was going to start looking for a job since I wasn't quite ready to retire. I just had no idea what since this very small town was not exactly the land of opportunities. She mentioned a 4-H coordinator position that was vacant. She thought I would be perfect for it. Later that evening, she emailed me the website to apply for it.

I read through the job description and ran it by Lucas. I had no real idea what this job entailed from the job description. *How hard could it be?* I had a college degree and have held some high-level corporate sales positions. Lucas encouraged me to apply for it. "Try something new" seemed to be his current motto.

Over the next few days, Katey and I got together frequently. We rode her horses and talked about our lives and how different they were to this point. She had had a tough childhood very different from my privileged one. She grew up in a small single-wide trailer and from an early age, Katey had been responsible for splitting all their firewood, which was their only source of heat. I would be afraid of getting hurt doing that. She and her husband, Scott, got married right out of high school. College had not been an option. There simply was no money for that. When her girls were little, Katey worked as a meat cutter for a butcher in town. *Wow,* I thought, *a woman doing that?* She also told me many stories about how poor they had been. For instance, when her girls were babies, there were times when they had to decide to purchase diapers or food. They simply could not afford both. I could not imagine that, but was developing a deep respect for this woman. She has had horses her whole life and, for most of that time, has been solely responsible for them.

Some of the things involved were moving eighty-pound bales of hay around the barn daily and trimming the horse's feet in the winter since they could not afford a farrier all year long. She did put shoes on them during the main riding season though. Katey and Scott still live in the same single-wide trailer that Katey grew up in, and they raised their girls there. Scott works long hours at the mill in town, and Katey now works in a dentist's office in town in addition to her horse boarding and training business on the side. They are extremely hard-working people and have raised their girls with those same attributes.

One morning, about a week after I met Katey, she called me and asked what my plans for the day were.

"Nothing in particular. Why? What's up?"

"Good. I'm coming to pick you up in about thirty minutes. We are going to the produce stand in town and then by the grocery store to pick up a few things. Then we are going to make green chili salsa and can it at your house because mine is too small."

"OK." I was game and always ready to learn something new.

We arrived back at our place around 9:30 in the morning. We chopped tomatoes and peppers all morning. Then we started cooking the salsa, using every pot, pan, and burner in my little apartment kitchen. Next, we filled the sink with hot water and started submerging all the pint jars Katey had brought. She was great at explaining why we were doing everything, step by step. Since there were forty-two pint jars, we had to work in batches. We then started filling each jar with salsa and processing them, seven jars at a time. We were now out of counter space, so I grabbed an eight-foot folding table from Lucas's shop and set it up in the living room. By 4:15, we had forty-two pints of salsa.

It had been a long tedious process, but standing there looking at those finished salsa jars, which would last all winter, I was so proud of what we accomplished and what I learned. I could not wait to show Lucas. I was not sure I was ready to can anything by myself yet, but it was not as hard as I had expected—just a lot of work. *Who knows. Maybe someday I will have a big garden and can a bunch of our produce for winter.*

The more I got to know Katey, the more I continued to be in awe of her. I would frequently be at her place when it came time to feed the horses. I would help where I could. It was always an education. I was learning a ton about horses.

One day, I was struggling to move an eighty-pound bale of hay in the barn. I, somehow, needed to get it up on top of three other stacked bales. I could barely lift it. At five feet nine, I have always been strong and athletic, but this was different. The baling twine was cutting into my fingers, and the whole bale was just awkward to lift. Katey is about five feet three and I would not have said as athletic as me until I witnessed her take that bale out of my hands and in one fell swoop, lift it over her head and stack it on top like she was in a strong man competition. I was shocked. How did she do that? Apparently, farm-strong and gym-strong are two entirely different things.

One afternoon in October when I was with Katey, her youngest daughter, now a junior in high school, came home from school, changed into camo, grabbed a rifle, and told her mom she was going deer hunting. With that she proceeded to walk off into the woods, rifle over her shoulder, by herself. I was flabbergasted that a woman, much less a young girl, would go off and hunt for deer by herself.

"Wow. She hunts for deer? And all by herself?"

"Yea. She has done that since she was twelve years old. She skins and cleans them herself also," Katey said proudly.

The women in Bonners Ferry were turning out to be a different breed than the women I had known all my life in Virginia. They were not better or worse—just different. They were strong, confident, and seemed completely self-sufficient from a young age.

Katey and Scott were raising their girls to be just that. They did not want them to ever have to rely on anyone to take care of them. I was so impressed by this. In addition, those girls were absolutely gorgeous and honor society students in high school.

On another afternoon, I stopped by to help feed the horses. Scott was in the driveway.

"Hey, Scott. Is Katey in the barn?"

"No. She is in the garage changing the shocks on her truck because *she* wanted to do it *herself*," he replied with a hint of frustration in his tone.

"What?" was all I could say.

"Go on in," as Scott motioned to the garage.

I walked in and what I saw completely flummoxed me. Katey was lying on one of those rollie boards, half under the front of her truck. Her shirt was up to her chest and her entire belly was exposed.

"WHAT are you doing?" I asked.

She rolled out from under the truck, tugged her shirt down and said, "Oh, hey," like it was any other normal day.

All I could think of at that moment was . . . I don't even know how to put it into words. I just started laughing, and I could not stop as she looked at me bewildered, like something was wrong with me. Out of all the women I had known in my life, it never would have occurred to me that any of them would be changing the shocks on their vehicle, ever.

"What the heck?" I finally managed. "You really do continue to amaze me."

If this was an example of how most of the women in this county were, I was not sure if I would ever fit in.

· · · · **·** · **·** · · ·

Around that same time, Lucas and I had already met another couple, also neighbors, whose property was right next to ours, Jen and Rusty. Jen and Rusty were also friends with Katey and Scott. Rusty convinced Lucas that we had to have a side-by-side. A side-by-side is like a cross between a four-wheel ATV and a jeep—similar to a golf cart on steroids with bigger tires. Since Lucas was always looking for the next adventure, he was not too hard to convince. Katey and Scott had one, and it seemed everyone around here had them. They were street-legal, except for the highway. So, we bought a four-seater Kawasaki Teryx, thinking that this could be a fun thing to do when friends or family came to visit us.

By now, it was fall, and even though we did not have all the colorful trees like the East Coast, we did have a deciduous pine tree called a Larch or Tamarack. Its needles turned a brilliant shade of yellow before falling off in the fall. They tended to blanket certain spots on the mountains, making a nice contrast of green and yellow. There were all types of new plants, bushes, and smells that could not be found on the East Coast. I had so much to learn about this area.

Jen and Rusty invited us to join them, along with Katey and Scott, one Saturday. They were going to trailer the side-by-sides to some place at the bottom of the Selkirk Mountains and spend the day riding up to the top, off-road. The plan was to have lunch at the top and then head back down. That sounded like fun and something new for us to try. We were certainly game.

As we drove out of our driveway that morning on our way to meet everyone, we noticed a mangy, feral-looking tabby cat sitting beside the driveway, watching us leave.

"I have never seen that cat before. Have you?" I asked Lucas.

"Nope. Huh," was all Lucas said.

We all met at the bottom of our driveway and followed each other to a parking area at the base of the mountains. I was excited to try this. It was something I had never even thought of doing in my prior life. Katey and Scott led the way in their side-by-side, followed by Jen and Rusty. Lucas and I were in the back. I quickly understood why in all those old westerns on TV, the cowboys wore bandannas covering most of their faces. The dust was unbelievable. We tried to stay back as far as we could and still see them, but we were still in a cloud of dust. About halfway up that mountain, our trail became very narrow with overgrown alder bushes on either side. I was constantly dodging the branches that were whipping at us. Still, many of them broke off and were all over the inside of the side-by-side. When we finally reached the top, after a total of about two and a half hours, I was pulling branches and twigs out of the inside of my jacket. Some were even sticking out of the top of my jeans in the rear. When Katey came out of the bushes, having had to use the little girl's room, she announced, "I have sticks and leaves where nobody should have them."

That made me laugh. Apparently, we all had twigs and leaves in our clothes. It had been fun getting there though, and it was time for lunch.

We brought some sandwiches. Katey and Scott brought a small camp grill and heated smokies for everyone. Jen and Rusty brought apple pie, moonshine, and beer. They explained it is a tradition to have a toast at the top of the mountain, which we all did. We spent about an hour on the top of Apache Ridge, which I now know is the name of that mountain. There were the most incredible 360-degree views. It was stunning, with all the yellow patches sprinkled among the green pine trees all over those mountains. It was such a clear sunny day. We could see for miles and miles in every direction, over the tops of other mountains. I truly felt like I was on the top of the world. The air felt so clean and fresh. I believed, in that moment, that sitting on top of a mountain like that was far more therapeutic than just about anything else.

On the way back down, we made a few detours and found an old dilapidated, one-room log cabin tucked away on the mountain. Somebody must have really wanted to be alone. There was even a metal box spring for a bed still inside. We came across a large sand hill dune that we took turns seeing if we could get to the top of in our side-by-sides. We found out a four-seater side-by-side couldn't do everything the two-seaters could. We still had fun though. When we began that day, I confess, I had no idea what to expect. By the time we got back to our cars, it was starting to get dark, and I felt a little disappointed that the day was over already. I had really enjoyed that.

Once we got home and I had a chance to look in the bathroom mirror, I was so surprised at how dark my face looked. Had I gotten a sun tan? Upon closer inspection, I realized there was dirt caked on my face as well as every other part of me that was exposed—a result of riding in the back of the line. After scrubbing myself in the shower and feeling so much cleaner, I noticed that my face itched a little. I tried not to scratch it and was sure it would be fine in the morning.

The next morning, while waking up in bed, I noticed my eyes felt a little puffier than normal. It was probably from sleeping on the side of my face. As I turned the light on in the bathroom and looked in the mirror, I was horrified. My entire face was so swollen that I did not even recognize myself. I no longer had a bridge on my nose. My eyes were so swollen that they stuck out as far as the bridge of my nose and they could barely open. My upper lip was now touching the bottom of my nose and my cheeks did not even look real. I had silver dollar-sized hives all over my neck and arms. *Oh my God! That surely could not be me in the mirror.* I was having some sort of out-of-body experience. I grabbed some Benadryl and walked out to the kitchen, where Lucas was sitting. He looked up from the book he had been reading and calmly said, "Oh Babe. We need to go see somebody."

"Ya think?" was all I could say, sarcastically.

"Yes, maybe a divorce attorney?" Lucas said with a laugh.

"That is not funny," I said as I almost burst into tears.

"It's okay. I'm sorry. Why don't you get dressed and we will run into the emergency room."

It turns out I had some sort of severe allergic reaction to something on that mountain. I went through two months of allergy testing, and no one could figure it out. It took almost two full months for the swelling in my face to go away, and I was taking a cocktail of

Benadryl, prednisone, and Clariton, all in large doses, prescribed by doctors.

Every time we went up into the mountains on side-by-sides after that, which was not often, I would make sure to completely cover my face in addition to riding in the front. I still had reactions, although never as bad as that first time. I was very wary of that happening again and eventually stopped taking the side-by-side into the mountains in the fall. That seemed to be the only time of the year it bothered me.

In the meantime, as soon as the swelling abated, it was time to start looking for that job. I was not quite ready to retire.

7

Finding A Job

B onners Ferry was not exactly the land of career opportunities. The entire county consisted of no more than 12,000 residents at that point. The downtown area was two blocks wide by two blocks long. We have one stoplight, are mostly agricultural, and are one of the poorest counties in Idaho. Having spent my whole professional life in corporate sales in a large metropolitan area, I was somewhat at a loss for what to do here. Aside from wanting to save for my retirement, so as not to depend on my husband for that, (I learned that lesson from my first marriage) I was looking forward to meeting new people here. What better way to do that, than finding something new to do?

Katey had suggested I apply for the 4-H County coordinator position. For some reason, she thought I would be a good fit. I had no agriculture or farming background and honestly knew nothing about 4-H. Nonetheless, I applied for that position as well as two others in the area—a clerical position in the courthouse and a sales position for a small newspaper in Sandpoint, which would have required an hour's commute each way.

I was surprised when I received three offers. None of them paid much or seemed to really excite me, but opportunities were limited here. Two of them did, however, offer a county retirement plan. I would have to take what I could get. Lucas strongly encouraged me to try something totally different since this was a brand-new chapter in our lives. So, I went with the 4-H coordinator position. I had no idea what I was getting into.

After accepting the position, I learned I would be largely responsible for the County Fair, which is the biggest event in the county. How hard can this be, right? After all, I have a college degree and have worked with some high-level clients in some very stressful situations in DC. I have always prided myself on working best under pressure. However, I knew next to nothing about farm animals, sewing, quilting, or Dutch oven cooking. Up until this point, I thought a Dutch oven was a double-boiler. But I was prepared to jump right in and learn. I had been to a handful of county fairs in the past and never paid any attention to the animal shows. I preferred to focus on live music and food. It was somewhat cleaner.

The night before my first day on the job, which happened to coincide with the first day of the County Fair, my new boss called to tell me to report at 7 a.m. to the animal barn at the fairgrounds to weigh in all the swine. Nothing like jumping right into a new career at the busiest week of the year. Talk about trial by fire. As I hung up the phone, I looked at my husband and repeated what she told me, asking, "Swine are pigs, right?"

"Oh boy," was all Lucas could reply, followed by that now familiar laugh somewhat under his breath.

I arrived at the animal barn early, at 6:45 a.m., wanting to make a good impression. I was prepared to learn how to weigh in a handful of, what I thought would be small, pigs. What I saw was another thing altogether—more like utter chaos. There were two hundred twenty very large pigs, all loudly trying to break away from their handlers, which were, for the most part, little kids with big canes. Some of those kids had to have weighed about half of what their pigs weighed, or less. Oh my gosh! I couldn't help but wonder what I had gotten into. Up until now, my entire professional career had consisted of dressing in suits or slacks with blazers and attending client lunches and board meetings. I was used to getting regular manicures and using expensive skin and make-up products.

Currently, my job entailed making sure the correct pigs were paired with the correct owners, getting those pigs on the scale, writing down the weights and ear tag numbers, and forwarding them to a table of 4-H leaders who were inputting everything into a database. Overwhelmed seemed like an understatement for what I was feeling at the time. I was amazed at how some of these kids, who obviously weighed way less than their pigs, were expected to get them from point A to the scale and then to the ultrasound machine to be evaluated for fat content and back to their stalls—all with the help of only a cane.

Once everything started, that morning became a blur of loud squealing pigs, people shouting weights and tag numbers and generally trying to keep up with everything while making sure none of the kids got hurt trying to steer their stinky pigs.

Close to three hours later, I was looking forward to going to the ladies' room and try to clean myself up a little. Even though I mostly stood there and wrote down the pig weights and ear tag numbers, I could not help but get pig poop on myself, and the stench now seemed like it was permanently embedded in my nose. I had pig poop all over my new cowboy boots and jeans. I used to think the Purdue chicken farms on the East Coast stunk when we would drive by them on the way to the beach every summer. They were no match for these guys. The grease they put on the pigs immediately after getting off the scale and before the ultrasound was now all over my hands. I could not seem to get the little pig hairs off my hands and face, including my lips. Note to self: never *ever* wear chapstick to a pig weigh-in.

Finally, the last pig was on the scale. But, wait, we were not done. Next came the lambs and goats followed by the steers, all needing to be weighed in too. Thankfully, there were not as many of these. It also went quicker because the kids seemed to be able to handle these animals a little better. After another hour and a half, we were finally done with the weigh-ins. I couldn't wait to tell my friends on the East Coast about this. I was fairly certain, after they initially had a good laugh, that a few of them would be on the next plane to Idaho to rescue me. They would want to know exactly what I had been thinking when I took this job.

The rest of that first day was not quite as eventful or memorable. I managed to get through it. That evening, thoroughly exhausted,

Lucas seemed most amused by my first day as 4-H coordinator. I had no idea what was in store for the rest of fair week.

Days two and three of that week were consumed with all of the animal shows. I lived in the animal barns. If I did not know anything about farm animals three days ago, I sure knew a lot more now. My days consisted of announcing all the animal shows and classes, which seemed to be endless. Admittedly, some of the kids, especially the smaller ones, were adorable trying to control their animals, especially the pigs, who never ceased to be anything by onery, always looking for an escape, or picking fights with other pigs.

On one occasion, an 8-year-old boy, half the size of his pig, trying desperately to control his animal with his cane, was knocked off his feet by the pig and ended up laying across the back of his pig while the pig spun in circles like a rodeo bull. It was cute and funny, while a little scary. I also remember the largest of the two hundred twenty pigs, which had to be close to three hundred pounds, was handled by an adorable eight-year-old girl. She wielded that cane like the Gestapo—not about to take any crap from that pig. I was so impressed. She had total control of him. I started to think that I might enjoy this job. It was going to be very entertaining, that was for sure.

When it came time to announce the steer shows, the papers I was given to read listed all the different shows by breed. I had no idea there were so many different breeds. Most of these breed's names were abbreviated. Not being familiar with all the breeds, other than Angus or Hereford, since that was mainly what we had on the East Coast, I prayed that I announced the names correctly. Even though Lucas had raised cattle for years before meeting me, I had no clue about all the different breeds.

I got through most of these shows fine. The only slip-up I had was the "Reg. Simentals." I announced "Regular Simentals" and the judge started to laugh in the middle of the arena in front of everyone. He looked over at me and said, "Abby, it's Registered Simental."

"Oh, okay." I looked over at my husband sitting in the stands, and he was just smirking and shaking his head, probably hoping no one knew I was his wife.

The days of fair week were exceptionally long, anywhere from twelve to eighteen hours each day. They were filled with lots of funny happenings. As I was opening the goat barn one morning, one of the larger La Mancha goats, the odd-looking ones with the tiny ears, was standing on his hindlegs happily munching away on the poster hanging over his pen that his 4-H kid had made and that gave all kinds of information on his goat. While the days were mostly centered around animal shows, the evenings entailed opening ceremonies, 4-H fashion shows, Family Fun Night, and the Animal Livestock Auction on Friday night. Based on the crowd that evening, it seemed the whole county must have shown up to support the local kids at that auction. It was heartwarming to see this.

During the auction, I sat next to the auctioneer and was to preside over this auction. This was the first auction I had ever been to in my life, and I was excited about it. Once things started rolling, boy did they move fast. I struggled to keep up with what was going on at times. Thank God for one of the sheep leaders who sat on the other side of me and was an old pro at this. She was a tremendous help. That was my longest day of the week; it started at 7 a.m., and I finally got home after 11:00 that evening.

I had to be back at the animal barn at 4 a.m. the next morning to help the meat processors mark all the animals as to where they would be going for processing the following day. We did this using different colored grease markers. We would put a red, blue, or green line on the sides of the pigs, goats, or sheep. The steers were done a little differently. I could not help but feel sorry for them all, even the onery pigs. I confess, I momentarily wondered what would happen if I accidentally left their doors open for them all to escape. The flip side of that was this was how many of these kids made a little money to put toward college, etc. It was a totally different lifestyle than I was used to—not bad, just different.

Later that morning, I worked the fowl shows and the kid's sales competition. I finished that day around 2:00 and went home, never feeling so exhausted in my life. I now understood the term "bone tired." Saturday night was Family Fun Night at the fair and the only event I was not required to attend. I could not wait to sleep, especially since I had to be back Sunday morning at 3:30 to help load up all the animals to go to various slaughter facilities. The leaders wanted the animals all gone before the kids showed up to clean the stalls. It was less upsetting for them. I understood that.

While I had sleep first and foremost on my mind, Lucas did not. I suppose he had a lot of downtime while I was working that week and was getting antsy. When I walked in the door, he said, in all seriousness, "Hey, let's go to Family Fun Night tonight and have some fun."

I stared at him in utter disbelief. Could he really be serious?

"Absolutely not," was all I could manage, while wondering if he was in his right mind. "I need to get away from that place for a little bit and sleep."

He was actually disappointed and ended up going without me. That was probably just as well since I fell asleep around 7:00.

I was back there at 3:30 a.m., helping to herd all those animals into their designated trucks to go to processing. I did not particularly enjoy that morning. The idea of what I was doing, or maybe it was my sheer exhaustion, made me feel sick to my stomach. There were five of us, four large, robust truck drivers and me, trying to load all the pigs into their appropriate trucks. The trucks were backed up to the barn doors with a ramp for the animals to climb inside. We used large boards to try to herd them. Several pigs wanted no part of this and escaped into the barn, trying to run and hide. I wondered how much those pigs understood about what was happening.

One of the truck drivers who was helping herd them had an electric cattle prod. He would zap those pigs, and their screaming was ear-piercing. It was a mess. Pigs were getting loose in the barn, squealing and pooping everywhere. Someone said they poop when they get stressed. I believe they are just pooping machines, pooping any and every chance they get.

On the other side of the pig barn were some goats. One goat kept untying the lead line that tied him to his pen, jumping over his gate, and running around the barn screaming. I kept putting him back, and he kept getting out again. He was a little Houdini. He was so cute, I wanted to take him home with me. I felt so sorry for him. All of this made me wonder if these animals knew this morning was not going to be a good one for them.

After we got all the pigs, lambs, and goats loaded, different stock trucks showed up for the steers. Surprisingly, they were the easiest of the livestock to load. As soon as the last steer was loaded, someone discovered that same little goat cowering in the corner of the barn. One of the handlers picked him up and threw him in the trailer with the steers. *That surely can't be safe for him.* Poor little guy almost made it out of there. I wanted to cry and was still a little sick to my stomach.

Once we were done, I headed home and took a long hot shower. I smelled like pig poop again and just wanted to be done with this week. This was definitely my least favorite day. I did not feel good, partly due to sheer exhaustion and partly due to feeling like I was the one sending all those animals to their end. I managed to fall asleep sitting in the shower at least twice that morning. When I was done, I crawled into bed. Just before I fell asleep, I noticed that same mangy tabby cat sitting on top of our hot tub outside the bedroom window. He was just staring at me as to say "I know what you did today."

What in the world is the rest of the year going to be like at this job? If it is anything like fair week, I will not make it six months. I dozed off and slept until mid-afternoon.

· · · ● · ● · · ·

That winter was filled with 4-H Leaders' Award Ceremonies, selling advertising for next year's fairbook to local businesses, finding new leaders for different 4-H groups, and tons of other preparations for the following year's fair. I could not believe how much work went on all year, planning for the annual fair.

In early spring, following my first fair week, we did the first pig weigh-ins for the following year's fair. We did two weigh-ins total, this one and the one right before fair. We had to ensure that all the pigs were at a healthy weight, among other things. There were two hundred plus of these pigs again. They were much smaller this time but still hard to control as they were extremely wiggly and solid muscle. I knew I was going to need help doing this, so I recruited my husband and my son Kevin, who was visiting that weekend.

Kevin, my youngest, was in his first year of college. Lucas had nicknamed him Mr. GQ because he was always perfectly dressed for every occasion, without so much as a hair out of place. Even on that day, Kevin had on a new pair of Carhartt pants, a jacket, and new boots. He had showered that morning and was ready to go. Lucas was wearing his usual well-worn denim overalls, which he had started wearing five out of every seven days since we moved here, and a Carhartt jacket. Luckily for me, Kevin and Lucas both have excellent senses of humor. While Kevin did not seem to be overly excited about helping with this, he was more than willing. Like me, Kevin had no previous experience with farm animals.

We showed up at the fairgrounds early that morning. Again, my job was to write down the pigs' weights, ear tag numbers, and the names of their 4-H kid in addition to taking photos of each kid with their pig. Lucas ran the scale. Kevin loaded the pigs on and off the scale, then helped Lucas ear tag them. Kevin was then supposed to hand the pigs back to the 4-H kid while I took their photos. Since there was no way most of these kids, nor one person alone, could hold on to one of these little wiggly buggers, Kevin got his workout in by helping almost every one of those kids hold on to their slippery squirmy pig. About five minutes into this process, Kevin was desperately trying to hold onto a pig for a little girl when the piglet decided it had to poop—all over the front of Kevin. Lucas and I could barely stop laughing at the look on his face. He was thoroughly appalled, and there was nothing he could do about it because there were two hundred ten piglets left to go.

Kevin ended up wrestling most of those pigs so we could at least get a picture with the pig and the kid somewhere in the same photo. By the time we were thirty minutes into this event, Kevin was covered in pig poop, but at least he was laughing. He had given up trying to stay clean.

Several hours later, we were almost done when one of the pigs got loose and ran into the parking lot. Talk about a rodeo. No less than twenty teenage boys were chasing this pig and trying to get a bucket on its head because that is apparently how you catch a loose pig. The theory is if you can get a bucket on its head, it will stop moving. I am not sure how well that worked. It seemed to take a literal pile of seven boys to tackle and get a handle on this piglet. I don't think Kevin will ever forget that day. I just hoped he would come back and visit again.

· · · ● ● · ● ● · · ·

Over the next several months, as we worked toward that summer's fair, I continued to be outside of my comfort zone with some of my required tasks. At one point, my boss told me I would need to arrange to have a vet in the parking lot all day and be prepared to assist him with testing all the fair fowl for avian flu. Obviously, we could not allow any infected birds on the fairgrounds with the healthy ones.

"Just exactly how do we do that?" I asked, curious.

"You just swab their throats and send off the culture."

In my mind, I pictured holding one of those chickens, turkeys, geese, etc., while trying to make them open their mouths and say "aah" with a large Q-tip in my hand, which was pretty close to how it was done too. The only difference was that I did not have to do anything except write the information down and make sure all the birds registered for the fair got tested.

Another part of the job was finding various people in the community to lead the different 4-H groups. It was not all about animals. There was sewing, quilting, dutch-oven cooking, dog training, scrapbooking, cake decorating, archery, woodshop, etc. Since Lucas had built a state-of-the-art woodshop, I managed to convince him and a friend to teach the woodworking class. Other than dog training, I knew nothing about quilting, sewing, scrapbooking, or any of the other various subjects. I did not know that people still quilted; I'd never known anyone interested in that in my little world in Virginia. I also had almost no interest in crafty types of things. My mother is an artist, and throughout my childhood, she was always trying to get me interested in some type of craft. Let me tell you, we tried them all before I was twelve years old. We tried candle-making, stained glass ornaments, knitting, crocheting, and decoupage—we even made potholders and ashtrays. The only crafty thing I seemed to be remotely interested in was making those creepy crawly things with the different colored goo and the electric oven. My mom rarely let me do that since I always made such a mess. I always preferred to be outside with my friends or playing sports.

I stayed at this job for a little over three years. Fair week never really got any easier, and I seriously burned out. In the end, I really was not cut out for that job. It was an awful lot for one person to handle. In addition, I still missed getting dressed up for work and having lunch meetings with clients. It was the unexpected funny and amusing times that kept me there, along with some of the wonderful people I met in the process. I learned a lot and met most of the people in the county through my 4-H coordinator position. I was amazed at how much the people and businesses in the county continually showed up to support the kids for the livestock auction. Most of the kids in our county who went to college paid their way, and by purchasing their animals, the community helped with this expense. There were many times during these auctions that the families and local businesses would intentionally bid up some of these kids' animals way high just to help them out. There was such a sense of community here. That was something I never experienced in Virginia, at least not like this. The adage, "It takes a village to raise a child," came to mind on more than one occasion. This small-town feel was becoming such a welcome change. *Maybe I will like living here after all.*

8

Copper

One great thing that came out of my time as 4-H coordinator, was all the people I met. At one point that first year, Jeff Abernathy contacted me. This gentleman was looking to rehome three horses and wondered if there was anyone in 4-H who may be interested. Since we had just begun looking for horses, Lucas and I decided to ride down to Cocollala and look at them. Jeff had three Missouri Fox Trotters of various ages.

As soon as we arrived, it was obvious all three of those horses had been well taken care of. They appeared well-fed and groomed. Their feet indicated they had regular visits from a farrier, and their field and barn were clean and tidy. Jeff was a middle-aged man with short salt-and-pepper hair and glasses who owned an Insurance Agency in Sandpoint. He was very friendly. All three of these horses had been with him since birth. The youngest was five, a mare named Stella, who had never had a saddle on and was the first one to walk right up to us. She had been born there. Her mother died the previous winter. Stella was very green but sweet. The middle one was named Copper and had been this gentleman's wife's horse, and she had, sadly, passed away. He was copper colored and very gentle. The older horse, Shaker, was a paint and Jeff's horse. He was actually Stella's grandfather. All three horses were sound and had calm demeanors. Being new to riding, I was most interested in Copper. Stella was too green and Shaker was older. He had a wonderful demeanor, but I was afraid of getting too attached and then losing him too quickly. Copper seemed to be the obvious choice. Lucas and I took Copper and Shaker out for a little ride. Copper was fantastic. I loved his gait and slow lope. He was very well trained, and I hardly had to cue him with my legs.

From that first meeting, I felt Copper would be perfect for me. I can't explain how I knew that—call it a gut feeling. I prayed Lucas would agree with me.

For years, I had been anxiously awaiting the day I would get my first horse. Riding had become something I loved to do so much; I would fall asleep at night thinking about riding. When we got back to the barn, Lucas started talking to Jeff, and before I knew it, they had agreed on a price, and the deal was done. I was getting my first horse. This was an absolute dream. I felt like I was about to burst with emotions. They both looked over at me and for some reason, I burst into tears. They were happy tears. Lucas and Jeff looked surprised and were speechless. Through the tears, I apologized and said, "I can't help it. I have been waiting for this day for so many years, and he is perfect."

Once those tears started, they were hard to stop. While Lucas was surprised by my reaction, Jeff got teary-eyed himself. I felt as excited as any little girl getting her first horse. What a dream come true, and I had Lucas to thank for making this happen. We ended up bringing all three of those horses home that day. It was a day I will remember for the rest of my life and a day that would change my life forever.

· · · ● · ● · · · ·

We got them home and let them settle in. Lucas had a couple of saddles and a halter, but we were going to need to purchase some more tack before we could think about riding them. Katey offered to take me down to Garfield, Idaho, a little over an hour away, to a place where she likes to buy her tack at good prices. That sounded good to me.

I picked her up around 7:30 on Saturday morning. As we were driving down our road, toward Highway 95, I had to stop the car at one point. There were two random wild looking goats standing in the middle of the road. One looked like a large La Mancha goat—the type with extremely small ears. The other was much smaller and a different breed. They were filthy and matted and were standing still in front of us, staring at my car. I started to laugh.

"Only in north Idaho, would there be stray goats blocking a road," I said, as I laughed. I kind of thought they were cute.

"Ah, you better move your car."

"What? Why? I have to get a picture," I said, as I was fumbling with my phone. "No one in Virginia will believe this."

"Ah, you better move your car NOW!" Katey said, raising her voice.

"What?"

With that, those goats jumped up on the front hood of my car. The large funny-looking one was looking right at us and the little one was looking off to the side.

"Oh My God," was all I heard myself say, as I laughed even harder, still trying to get a picture of this.

"They are going to ruin the front of your car," Katey said, raising her voice, as she got out her passenger side door and started chasing them off my car.

She shooed them off the road and I immediately noticed several dents and scratches where they had been standing. It didn't matter. I could not stop laughing. Katey just looked at me, rolled her eyes, and shook her head as if I was a silly city girl. That made me laugh even harder. I think I laughed all the way to Garfield.

It was a successful trip, and I was able to purchase most of what we needed to start riding. At one point on the way home, Katey looked at me and said, "Would you please stop pumping the gas? I am going to get sick."

"I do not pump the gas," I said, indignantly. "Lucas says I do that. Huh."

"Okay," was all Katey said, as she rolled her eyes—again.

I tried to make a conscious effort not to do that the rest of the way home.

· · ● ● · ● ● · ● · ·

About a month after bringing those horses home, we decided to take them exploring in the forest service area behind our property. We were going up the side of a mountain with no visible trails. Lucas and I were trying to cut a new trail when, suddenly, Copper stopped walking and refused to go another step. I gently kicked him, trying to urge him on, but he did not move. My husband was getting impatient and said, "Kick him harder."

Lucas had been riding horses all his life and had more of a cowboy philosophy when riding. He believed in making a horse do what you want. I preferred a softer touch and tried to understand what Copper wanted to communicate in this situation. I wanted to build a mutual trust, not fear. I instinctively knew Copper would not stop for no reason. So, I got off him and started to check his feet. Sure enough, one of his back legs was tangled in vines. He was stuck. Some horses would have flipped out at this. Not Copper. He just stood patiently, waiting for me to figure it out. Once I got him unstuck, we were on our way. I love this horse!

Copper and I had some wonderful trail rides in the mountains of north Idaho and he always took good care of me. That first year, I rode Copper every chance I got, even if it was for only thirty or forty-five minutes at a time. At the very least, I would spend time with him every day, either grooming him, cleaning his stall and feeding him, or doing basic groundwork with him. He didn't appear to need much training. He seemed to know how to do everything. I believe he taught me much more than I taught him.

· · ● ● · ● ● · ● · ·

Around that time, Copper and I were invited to join a drill team. Drill teams consist of a group of riders, usually girls, who put a routine together to music. They normally perform just before a rodeo starts, right before the cowboy or cowgirl rides out with the American flag for the National Anthem. It is a way to get the crowd fired up. I was flattered and asked the woman, who was a friend of Katey's if she thought I was a good enough rider. She told me that she thought so and that the some of the other girls on the team were not as good as I was. I agreed to join and was excited to try something new with Copper.

At our first meeting, I met the other seven girls on this drill team. I realized I was the oldest by about thirty years. The youngest was twelve years old. I guessed they must've had a hard time finding an eighth rider when they invited me. That was okay with me. This drill team was very informal. We were only supposed to open for small schooling shows and rodeos, nothing too major. I felt it could be fun and may even improve my riding. In addition, Copper and I would learn something new together.

That spring, we started meeting a couple of times a week at the fairgrounds to put our routine together with music. Since there were eight of us, we did everything in pairs. Copper seemed to love this and learned the routines faster than me. Almost everything we did in our routine, was at a run. I was definitely improving my riding since I was thinking more about where I should be, instead of *We are running very fast and I could get hurt.* Even though I was comfortable running on Copper, once in a while that old voice in my head would creep back in allowing the fear of running on a horse to rear its ugly head. I was doing my best to suppress it.

One day, a woman was there watching us. At the end of our practice, she approached our coach and invited us to open for the Bonners Ferry Bull Bash, the largest rodeo event in our county. This is a huge event. The girls were all so excited they could barely contain themselves, so we said yes. As the lady turned to leave, she said, "Y'all better be good."

No pressure. Right? We were only supposed to open for smaller schooling shows, nothing too formal.

· · · · •·•· · ·

The big day finally came. It was Friday evening and time for the Bull Bash. We had worked tirelessly for weeks perfecting our routine. Lucas was back in Virginia visiting family and would miss the big event. However, my good friend Jennifer was visiting, and she would be there for everything. I remember thinking it was perfect because Jennifer is the best horseperson I have ever met. She grew up riding and used to exercise horses at Churchill Downs. There is nothing she was not capable of doing on a horse, and I mean nothing. She had been the first person to get me on a horse bareback, help me find my balance, and connect with my horse better. When I participated in schooling shows back in Virginia, she would help me bathe and groom my horse the night before. The morning of the show, she was there bright and early following Comet and me around with a brush sticking out of the back pocket of her jeans, for whenever he needed a touch-up in between classes. I had learned a ton from her and was so relieved she was here now.

I arrived home from work that day, changed into our uniform black cowboy shirt, hat, buckle, jeans, and boots and went down to the barn. We got Copper cleaned and loaded him in the trailer. I had been excited and stressed about this all day to the point where I couldn't eat any lunch. I suppose I must have had a little anxiety. Since Copper and I tend to feed off each other's emotions, he was a little high-strung also. We had a fifteen-minute ride to the fairgrounds. The whole way there, my heart was racing. I kept telling myself *this is not such a big deal. What is the worst that can happen?* I kept trying to remember to breathe and relax. It was not working. As we pulled into the fairgrounds parking area, I was immediately taken aback by how many cars were there. There were more cars than at any time during the fair. *Holy Cow!*

By the time I pulled Copper out of the trailer, he was dripping wet with sweat, his eyes and nostrils were as big as I had ever seen—all obviously anxiety since it was not even hot outside. All around us, there were cowboys swinging ropes, loading scary bulls being loaded into chutes, and cowboys warming up a bunch of horses in the arena along with loud music and stands full of people. "Oh Boy!" Our drill team coach took one look at Copper and asked, "Did you already warm him up?"

"Uh no, he just got off the trailer like that," I replied.

"Would you like me to warm him up for you?"

I must have had that dear-in-the-headlights look on my face. I gladly said, "Yes, please."

Beyond thankful for her help, I was relieved when she told me, "He is fine, just not big on the scary bulls in their chutes."

At that point, one of the other girls on the drill team approached me and told me she had lavender oil. I asked her what that was for and she explained, "If you put it inside the horses' nostrils, it will calm them down."

I did not even have to think about that. I quickly replied, "Yes. Go for it," wondering if it might work on me also.

I believe the only result was that Copper snorted a few times. Otherwise, it didn't seem to have any effect.

I then rode Copper into the arena so we could warm up together. *Maybe this will not be so bad after all.* The very next moment, one of the horses from our drill team ran by Copper and me without a rider. *That can't be good.* I turned around to discover that another horse from our drill team had kicked the rider off; she was five months pregnant. *Holy hell!!!* She ended up going to the hospital five minutes before our performance was due to start. My friend Jenn was left holding her horse. Things were starting to get tense. I could see it in each one of the other riders' faces.

Now seeing my way out of this, I happily offered, "Since we are doing everything in twos and we now have an odd number, I am happy to sit out if you all want to do this without me."

My heart was racing, and I could hear every beat like a bass drum in my head. By the looks of those stands, everyone in the county was there. At this point, I just wanted to go home and have a drink. What had I gotten myself into? Maybe this wasn't my best idea ever. I had a pit in the bottom of my stomach and was close to throwing up. My head was throbbing. However, the other girls were not having any of that. They said they needed me and that was that. It was not up for discussion. *Darn!* The last thing I wanted to do was let the girls down.

So there we went. Those stands were packed with people cheering us on. The music started and we entered the arena in pairs, at a run. We were supposed to run one whole lap around the arena and then go into our routine. Copper and I were between Amber on her horse on our left and the huge crowd of people roaring in the stands on our right. Copper was not digging any of this. Did I also mention that I had the only Missouri Fox Trotter among all of the quarter horses on the drill team? Fox Trotters have a gait that quarter horses don't have. It's a fast gait but looks entirely different from a lope. It is way fancier. Instead of running as we should have, we were doing our crazy sideways fancy, prancy gait the entire length of the crowd.

"Come on Copper, you've got this," I softly pleaded with him.

Once we got past the crowd, I got Copper back on track with everyone else. If that was the worst of tonight, then it was behind us. I tried to put that out of my mind and focus on going forward. After all, I have even seen horses act up at the beginning of the Kentucky Derby. By the end of the race, no one remembered that part. Maybe this would be no different.

Things seemed to be going well until about three-quarters of the way through the routine. We were doing our figure eight pattern, running and crossing in the middle, just barely missing each other. Timing was key here. Suddenly, Copper had had enough. Right in the middle of the figure eight, he planted his feet and came to a dead stop, facing the stands and refusing to move. *Oh, no you don't*, I thought as I kept trying to get him to move. I kicked him and kicked him, but he just stood there, facing the crowd.

"Oh, Copper, please don't quit on me right now," I pleaded with him.

He would not budge. My worst fears were happening. The other riders were swerving to miss us. I was more than slightly mortified. Over the loudspeaker, the announcer said, "Timing is everything, girls." *Ugh!*

I wanted to die! It was like Copper was saying, "That's it, this is too much for me." We stood like that for what seemed like an eternity. Talk about life's most embarrassing moments. This was it, and I was sure I would never recover. We stood like that, facing the crowd, while the drill team finished the routine.

I managed to get Copper to join at the end of the line for our final lap running around the arena and out into the holding pen. Once in the pen, I jumped off Copper, placing him between me and the stands, and burst into tears that I had been desperately trying to hold back. I was so embarrassed and felt bad for letting the team down. I looked next to me and there was Amber, crying because her horse was the one that kicked the other girl off her horse.

At that moment, the 6-foot-five cowboy carrying the American flag for the National Anthem rode right by us on his way into the arena and slightly spooked Copper with that big flag. He looked down at us from his large, stocky rodeo horse and gave us a humph of disgust. Oh boy, was I glad my husband was not there, even if the rest of the county was. I was never going out in public again. And to top it off, I was way older than every other girl on that drill team. In theory, I should've been a better rider.

I walked Copper over to the trailer, and Jenn met me there. She asked if I wanted to put Copper up and go watch the rodeo as if I would show my face in those stands tonight.

"No! I just want to go home," I whined, feeling more than slightly mortified and with a few tears still burning my eyes.

On the way home, Jenn looked at me and said, "I'm your friend, right?"

"Yes, of course," I replied.

"Well, that isn't a horse for a drill team, and you really aren't a rider for the drill team."

"Ya think?" was my quick cynical reply. At that moment, I agreed with her. "I can cross that one off my bucket list, and I promised Copper I would never make him do anything like that again. He was such a good sport. He could have totally acted up. Instead, he just shut down when it all became too much."

We drove home. After changing into our PJs and decompressing a little, we enjoyed a nice evening on the back porch with a much-needed bottle of wine while I contemplated how I would ever show my face in public again.

· · · · ● · ● · · ·

Despite that event, Copper became what some people call a once-in-a-lifetime horse. The bond between us grew quickly. We spent time together every day and rode whenever weather and time permitted. Unfortunately, I was only able to ride him for a few years.

When he was twenty-two, he developed arthritis in his rear hock. In those years he taught me so much and gave me so much confidence with riding. He is still with me, although retired, and will be with me until his last breath. He is my forever horse. The memories we made and the experiences we had in the few short years before he became lame are wonderful and unforgettable. I learned to put my total trust in him and he in me. From a lot of trail riding to riding in parades, briefly being part of a drill team, and opening for the county's largest rodeo, we did everything we could together. Some things were more memorable than others. We rode all over the mountains in north Idaho. He is now spoiled and loved on every day. I have never felt a bond with an animal like I do with him.

For a short time, I had a baby mule that I was going to attempt to work with and train—another thing on the bucket list. He turned out to be much more of a handful than I anticipated. After he managed to kick me in the forehead when I was attempting to pick up his feet, I became scared of him, and that was over. Until we found him the perfect home, there were occasions when I had to go into the pen to feed Copper and him. That baby mule liked to run by me while kicking out his back feet in my direction. Sometimes those feet got a little too close for comfort. I was always wary of that little bugger, and Copper knew it. Would you believe Copper consistently placed himself between that onery baby mule and me? I swear he was protecting me. I know it down in my bones. He has been loyal to me in a way most people could not be, and I love him even more for that.

9

Book Club

By the fall of that first year, I had met a handful of women I could now call friends. One of them, Amy, invited me to join a book club she was part of. I met Amy through her husband, Sean, who I had recruited to lead the 4-H dog training group. Lucas and I became instant friends with them. They had both retired from law enforcement in California and recently moved to Bonners Ferry. Sean had worked with the K-9 unit and was a perfect choice for helping 4-H kids train their dogs. He had one of those larger-than-life personalities and was hilarious. People were drawn to him. In addition, Amy was one of the sweetest people I had ever met.

Even though I enjoyed reading, I had not done any recreational reading since I met Lucas. Maybe this would get me back into it. Lucas also thought it would be a good way to meet some more people, so he encouraged it.

There were a total of twelve wonderful women in this group. At my first meeting in September, I spent a lot of time talking to a woman named Fiona. Everyone called her Fi, for short. She seemed very intelligent and had been an English teacher at the local high school. She was born and raised in Bonners Ferry. I guessed she was around my age, fifty-three, or so. We both enjoyed gardening. She was a widow, lived alone, and said she preferred it that way. We realized we did not live far from each other and decided to carpool to future book club meetings.

The women in this group were all very interesting, warm, and welcoming. There was Denise, a retired college English professor; Claire, a retired librarian; an author named Martha, who had just published her first book, and several other women who had retired from various careers, including law enforcement and nursing. Most of these ladies had moved from California after retiring and were close to my age. One of my favorite ladies I met that night, although I liked them all, was Debbie. I believe Debbie was in her late seventies and was the sweetest, most energetic, upbeat person there. She was originally from Canada but married a career US Marine and has lived all over the US. I knew from the first night that I was going to enjoy being part of this group.

For our October book club meeting, Fi asked me if I would mind driving. She preferred not to drive in the dark anymore if she did not have to. I told her I would be happy to drive and arranged to pick her up around 4:50 p.m. She gave me directions to her place. I hoped I wouldn't make her carsick.

It was almost dark when I pulled off the road and onto her driveway. Halfway up the driveway, I noticed a small fenced garden area and a few solar panels off to the side. Next, I noticed a chicken coop and a huge pile of wood that looked like it needed to be split. There was an ax sticking up on the top of a tree trunk, giving the impression someone had recently been splitting wood. Fi's house was just beyond that. As I pulled up to the small log home with a metal roof and several additional small outbuildings, all surrounded by large pine trees, Fi opened the front door and motioned for me to come in. I parked the car, walked up the porch steps made of logs that had been split horizontally, and stepped inside the house. My first impression of her house was that it was extremely neat, clean, and uncluttered. There was a small kitchen, living area, bedroom, and bathroom. The entire house could not have been one thousand square feet.

Fi was almost ready to go when she quickly ran back into the bedroom to grab something. As I stood in the kitchen, I noticed she had an old, wood cookstove in her kitchen that had wood burning in it. I also noticed that it was her only stove or oven. It reminded me of something my great-grandmother might have used. I thought that was interesting and wondered if she actually cooked on it. She did not have any kitchen cabinets but just a few shelves holding four dishes, four glasses, four coffee mugs and various pots and pans. There were two whole shelves lined with mason jars full of produce she must have canned from her garden. Everything was very neatly stacked. In front of the large white kitchen sink, curtains covered up what was under the sink. When she came back, I asked, "Where is your refrigerator?"

"I don't have one."

"What? How do you keep stuff cold?"

"I have a root cellar for some things, and I don't buy most things that need to be refrigerated. I live off-grid. It is a lifestyle you get used to. I have been doing this for about ten years now. I prefer it. I don't like having monthly bills if I can help it."

I had never met anyone who lived off-grid and did not have a good understanding of what all that entailed, but I was curious.

"Off-grid? I saw the solar panels. Do you use those for energy?"

"Yes. For my few electricity needs. I heat the house in the winter with my woodstove as well as cook on it, and there is an outhouse out back."

"Wow, you cook on that? Was it hard to get used to?" This impressed me, and I secretly wanted to learn how to do it myself to experience how my great-grandmother lived. I had always heard she was a fantastic cook.

"It took a little time, but I have been doing it for so long now, it's no big deal."

"You said you have an outhouse? What about showers?" I asked.

"Well, I do not have a well here, so I have to haul water from town about once a week."

I had noticed the large tank in the back of a pickup truck in her driveway.

Fi explained that she fills up a ten-gallon bucket of water, heats it on her woodstove, hoists it up outside, and pours it into another bucket with holes in the bottom.

"So, you have an outside shower, then?"

"Sort of." We walked outside and there was a four-by-four-foot wooden platform next to the house with the hoisting contraption next to it.

"So, the shower is not enclosed—at all?" I asked, with a hint of concern.

"No. I don't have any neighbors up here." She laughed. "The only time it can be a little uncomfortable is when it's really windy and cold," she said with a smile.

The longer we talked about this, the more questions I had. Fi seemed genuinely amused at my questions. I was starting to get a clearer picture of what living off-grid meant. I was so curious about how and why she was doing it but did not want to offend her by asking too many questions.

"So, who splits your wood for you?"

"I do." She said with a smile.

The women in this county never cease to amaze me. Here is this lady, almost sixty, looking extremely well put together, living completely off-grid, practically on top of a mountain, entirely alone, and she is truly happy living this life. Fi had plenty of money and certainly could afford to live in town. In fact, she had not always lived like this. She grew up in a small house in downtown Bonners Ferry. Her husband had always talked about living off-grid. Four months after they finally made that transition, he died unexpectedly. That was ten years ago. Fi has lived here ever since. I had a million questions for Fi, but they would have to wait. We needed to get going to book club.

• • • • • • • • • •

Everyone in our book club brought something to eat or drink to each meeting, and we spent most of the time doing just that while catching up on each other's lives. There was always plenty of wine and great food, as we were always trying to outdo each other with our homemade dishes and desserts. We would then spend about thirty minutes discussing that month's assigned book. I loved these get-togethers.

That evening, I walked into the kitchen at the clubhouse where we had our meetings to drop off my Caesar salad and overheard Debbie talking about her recent hunting trip with her family. Debbie was the oldest member of our book club.

"Oh yes, both my boys and my grandkids were there as well as my husband. We camped there for the weekend and had so much fun." I heard her say. "I managed to get a deer on the last day."

Wait. What? I was having a hard time wrapping my head around the fact that Debbie hunts. *Sweet, classy, little Debbie who my dad always sees in church?* They attend the same Catholic church in town. I could not contain myself any longer.

"Debbie, do you actually hunt?" I asked as everyone in the kitchen turned to look at me. I started to feel like my previous lifestyle was making me stick out like a sore thumb.

"Oh Yes. We've been doing this trip every year for the past fifteen years. We love it."

"Wow. I just had not pictured you shooting a gun." As soon as I said that, I regretted it. I sounded like a silly city girl, again.

That led to a discussion with the rest of the women about guns. I learned that every one of them carries a gun, and more than half of them either have hunted or still hunt regularly. When I pictured women hunting or living off-grid, these ladies were not at all who I pictured. Yet, here they were. By East Coast standards, they all appeared very normal to me, yet they were more outdoorsy, tough, and way more self-sufficient. I knew I could never shoot an animal, but strangely, I admired these women for being able to. Sometimes I felt like I was not only across the country from where I had lived, but in a different world.

On our way home from that meeting, Fi and I continued to talk about living off-grid. I was still having a hard time understanding why anybody would want to do it unless they had to. Once we got back to her house, I hated to ask, but I did, "Fi, do you think I could use your bathroom, uh outhouse? I don't think I am going to make it home." I had to pee so bad.

"Sure. Hang on one minute," she said as she ran inside the house to grab something.

She handed me a battery-powered lantern since it was dark and there was no power in the outhouse. She then handed me a large piece of Styrofoam with a hole cut in the middle of it. *What the heck?* Fi noticed my perplexed look and explained that since it was so cold out, I might want to use it as the toilet seat. She kept it in the house and carried it back and forth when needed, so it would not be so cold in the winter.

"Right. Okay," was all I could say. I think I would have felt better just going behind a tree.

10

Toby

A few years after we moved there and at least a year after we said goodbye to our last dog, Grady, we started thinking about getting another one. I was not sure I was ready.

Fi also volunteered at an animal shelter. We had become good friends, and she knew about me having to say goodbye to my last dog, Grady. That had been tough for me. She mentioned this young boxer that had just been dropped off at the shelter. While I always thought boxers were intriguing and comical, I just was not ready. I was still feeling the sting of losing Grady. Lucas and I share the same philosophy regarding dogs. We love them and prefer to have one at a time. Our dogs are part of our family and treated as such. We become so attached to them, some more than others, which always makes it difficult to have to say goodbye when that dreaded day eventually comes.

Grady was a goldendoodle and we had gotten him when my boys were little. He grew up with Billy and Kevin. Throughout the boys' childhoods, my divorce, the transition with Billy and Kevin leaving home and heading off to college, and remarrying Lucas, Grady had been my one constant, always by my side. About a year after moving, Grady was eleven, and his back legs eventually gave out on him. After taking him to see Dr. Derek, it was obvious he was declining rapidly. The humane thing to do was to say goodbye. I needed a few more days to wrap my head around it. I hadn't expected that day to come so soon.

When that morning came, I knew it was time, so I called the vet's office. As much as I loved Grady, and I loved him a lot, I could not let him suffer. Dr. Derek offered to come out to the house to do it, saying it was much less stressful for everyone, especially Grady. While we waited for him, Lucas went out and dug a small grave on a knoll at the bottom of our property that I had picked out. My dad also showed up for moral support. I spent all morning holding Grady, not wanting to believe that the day had arrived.

Once Dr. Derek showed up, he was quick. Grady died peacefully in my arms. Lucas picked him up and said he would take him out to bury him. I offered to go with him, but he said, "No, Abby. That is not something you need to be there for. I will come and get you when it is done."

I was grateful for that and obliged him. As Dr. Derek was leaving, with tears in my eyes, I said, "Wait. I need to pay you."

"Not now." He replied. "You can stop by the office later this week when you are in town and pay."

Having a small-town veterinarian who makes house calls at times like these, seemed to restore some of my faith in people. There really are good, kind, and considerate people out there. In addition, Lucas thought so much about my grief that it was enough to make me cry by itself.

Later that afternoon, Lucas walked down to Grady's grave with me. Unbeknownst to me, he had made a wooden cross and carved and burned Grady's name onto it. Lucas has got to be the kindest, most thoughtful person I know.

· · · ● · ● · ● · · ·

Several months went by and Fi contacted me again, saying, "I don't know if you are interested or not, but the same family just brought that same boxer back to the pound, and he is so sweet."

At the time, I was in Coeur d'Alene for two weeks, taking real estate classes. I was getting back into selling real estate and needed to get my Idaho license. I called Lucas to tell him about this boxer.

He just happened to be running errands and was a block away from the shelter, so he decided to go and look at him. Lucas called me that evening and told me he really liked that boxer. He just wanted to make sure I was ready for another dog. I told him I thought I was, and Lucas ended up going back the next morning to pick him up. I was so excited to meet him but still had three more days of classes. I would not be home until late Friday night.

On Thursday night, Lucas had a board meeting. He was on the board of our community water system. He was only going to be gone a few hours. He called me and said that Toby, our dog's new name, had been so good, he was thinking of leaving him loose. He was completely house-trained, very quiet, sweet, and overall, seemed like the perfect dog. However, I cautioned him, and we decided to leave him in the laundry room/mud room. It was a pretty good-sized room.

Several hours later, as I was sitting in my hotel room, doing my real estate homework for the day, I got a phone call from Lucas.

"I just sent you a text with a photo. Don't you dare laugh. I just got home, and you would not believe the mess in this laundry room. I don't even know where to start."

It turns out Toby had opened a bunch of Christmas packages that were just delivered. They were full of those biodegradable packing peanuts. Thousands and thousands of them were everywhere. Apparently, when mixed with liquid, they turn into a glue substance. Toby had also punctured several gallon-size water jugs and somehow managed to get the five-gallon container of liquid laundry detergent that I had just purchased from above the washing machine and spilled that all over everything. Now those melted packing peanuts were blue and stuck to the bottoms of Toby's feet and Lucas's shoes. There were so many stuck to Toby's feet that he stood about four inches taller. The only way Lucas could get them off Toby and his own shoes was to soak them in the bathtub for a while. In addition, Toby had pulled all the coats off of the coat rack on the wall, the ironing board was upside down, and he managed to shred a big piece of memory foam.

When I hung up the phone with Lucas and finally looked at that photo, I could not stop laughing. In fact, I laughed myself to sleep that night. I kept picturing that scene in *Turner & Hooch*, where the dog destroys everything, and Tom Hanks goes crazy. At the same time, I was not sure if Toby would still be there when I got home the next night or not. This was the first dog we had gotten together, and I wasn't sure how Lucas would handle this once he managed to get everything cleaned up. I had not even met Toby yet.

The next morning, I got a text from Lucas with a photo of Toby laying his head on Lucas's lap and the caption said, "He's sorry." So, Lucas turned out to be a bit of a softy. I was glad they had worked it out, and I could not wait to meet Toby. Lucas had called the shelter that morning, and it turned out they forgot to mention that Toby has some anxiety issues when left alone.

• • • • • • • • • • •

That Friday night, as I walked into the house, Toby got up off his bed and calmly, almost hesitantly, walked over to me, as if to say, "Hello." He did not jump around or get overly excited, nor did he bark. I got down on the floor, held his face in my hands, and said, "Well, hello there handsome. I am so glad you have joined our family."

I noticed his top lip on the right side of his face was caught in his bottom tooth. Yet, he had the most serious expression. He was so cute, and his expression made me laugh.

Over the next few weeks, Lucas bought a couple of different crates and kennels to use when we had to leave Toby home. The first one was the metal cage-like crate. We put him in it and went out to dinner on a Friday evening, totally confident it would contain Toby. When we came home, he greeted us at the door, wagging his tail so hard that his entire rear end looked as if it would break off from the rest of him. He had destroyed the crate. We had no idea how he managed to do that. In addition, the butter dish, which had been left on the kitchen counter with a new stick of butter on it, was now in the laundry room and licked clean. I had no idea what that was going to do to his digestive system.

Since the weather was warm, Lucas decided to build him an outside dog kennel. He purchased six-foot chain link fencing panels and assembled them up against the side of our house. The first time we put him in it was when Lucas wanted to take a family who was visiting up to the back of our property and teach them how to shoot guns. He set a target up and spent about thirty minutes up there. I went along and watched, still not wanting anything to do with guns. When we got back to the house, again, Toby greeted us at the door, furiously wagging his tail. How he had gotten inside completely perplexed us until we went downstairs to the guest room and noticed that we had left the window open with a screen in it. That window opened up inside of the dog kennel on the side of the house. Apparently, after hearing gunshots, Toby jumped through the window, bending and breaking the screen in half.

After that, Lucas purchased a large plastic crate with no metal bars. It was our last resort. We put blankets in the bottom of it and, thankfully, this one seemed to work although we rarely left him behind.

Despite all of that, I fell in love with this guy so fast. Lucas got even more attached, quickly. Toby was so different from any other dog I have ever had. He was calmer and yet he was only two years old. Whenever we were in the house, he would go right to his bed and lie there until we went out again. At first, he was hesitant to play with any toys even though we had a basket full for him. We felt a little sorry for him and wondered how bad the first two years of his life had been. Every time we would try to touch the top of his head, he would wince and shy away. I believe that at first, Toby wondered when we were going to take him back to the shelter. That was never going to happen. We continued to show him lots of love and treat him like family.

A few months after Toby had settled in, Lucas had to fly back to Virginia for a few days. While he was gone, I allowed Toby to sleep in the bed with me. Lucas never allowed this when he was home. Toby had his own bed on the floor next to ours. However, having Toby next to me made being alone in the middle of the wilderness a little more comfortable. That first night, I coaxed him up on the bed with me, rolled over on my side away from him, and turned off the light. He settled down, lying up against me with his head lying on top of my head. He was taking his job as "protector" very seriously, and I felt totally safe. *If this isn't loyalty, I don't know what is.*

We took him everywhere we could. That was easy because he was so calm and good in public. Lucas worked on training him on and off-leash. We got to the point that we could take Toby to Home Depot, and without a leash, he would not leave Lucas's side. We really could take him anywhere. He would sit in the back seat of the car and look out the window. He never jumped around in the car or got carsick. We took him to Yappie Hours in Sandpoint and to visit elderly people at assisted living facilities. At the assisted living facilities, Toby would just walk up to residents and lay his head on their laps. They usually made a big fuss over him. We took him to parades, which he seemed to absolutely love. He would sit next to Lucas on the sidewalk and wag his tail at everything that went by. Lucas even built him his own seat in the back of our side-by-side. Toby became such a big part of our lives that every decision we made seemed centered around him. Lucas started saying that if Toby was not welcome somewhere then he did not want to go. That may seem a little extreme, but that is how special this guy was. Everybody loved him.

· · · ● · ● ● · · ·

A few months after Toby came to live with us, I took him for my regular five-mile walk. We walked to the end of our road, a few miles down the next road, and back. These are dirt and gravel roads, with only a few farms spread out off them. There was not much traffic. I would usually keep Toby on a leash unless we were within a mile of our house. Once we were that close, the only traffic would be Lucas or I or my parents, so I normally let him run off leash.

On our way back that day, we were about three-quarters of a mile from home; I had forgotten to unhook Toby's leash when I noticed something move out of the corner of my eye. I turned, looked again, and saw it was a huge mountain lion. He had been lying a little off the side of the road and was now getting up and staring right at me. I could feel my adrenaline spike to an all-time high. My first thought was, *This is how I am going to die. I am going to be attacked by a mountain lion.* Then another thought raced through my head. *No one will hear me if I scream.* Instinctively, something told me not to run, and I did not want to take my eyes off this cat. My cell phone would not work as with so many places around there. Toby never barked. Instead, he pressed up against my leg as we continued walking. I later questioned if he saw the mountain lion or if he was reacting to my heightened anxiety. They say dogs can sense our anxiety. By then, I was almost walking backward, watching this lion intensely watch me.

Just then, a pickup truck pulled out of our driveway just ahead of us. It was Jake, from the Forest Service. I had forgotten Lucas was meeting with him that morning. Jake was in his mid-forties and had lived his entire life in this area. He had that laid-back, good ole boy personality, like so many of the local guys. I frantically waived him down and told him about the mountain lion, who was now, nowhere to be seen.

"No shit," Jake said. "Well, it is a good thing you had your dog with you. That probably saved you since they use dogs that look like yours to hunt those lions."

I was so rattled by this that before Jake knew it, Toby and I were climbing into the back seat of his truck, moving all his various tools to the other side. I made him take us back to our house before he left. I was never walking Toby by myself again.

I found Lucas in his shop, and told him about this frightening ordeal. It was not that Lucas did not believe me, but he did not seem to consider it to be as big of a deal as I did.

"Why are you not more concerned about this? I could have been killed." His cool, calm demeanor was starting to annoy me.

"Abby, there are mountain lions here. There are grizzlies, moose, wolves, and all kinds of other wild life. It is a part of where we live. Mountain lions are always here. However, they are usually so elusive that you may never see one again. Besides, when was the last time you heard of somebody getting killed by a mountain lion?"

"But, Lucas, I am afraid to walk my dog now. And since I was already uncomfortable riding my horse off our property alone, in case I have an accident or run into a grizzly bear, I definitely won't do that either, now."

"We will figure something out, Abby. Maybe you should carry a gun, or at least bear spray, or something, when you walk."

Lucas knew I didn't want to carry a gun. Two days later, he came home from town with a small container of pepper spray. It was small enough to fit in the palm of my hand. That would help my confidence a little. However, I was still not walking Toby or riding my horse, off our property alone. No way!

• • • ●•●•● • • •

A couple of mornings later, as I was walking into the kitchen, I noticed Toby sitting in front of the kitchen door, intently staring at something. It was not like he was asking to go out. This was different. I walked over to him and looked out the window. There was that mangy tabby cat, sitting on the outdoor sofa like he did not have a care in the world.

I had started putting some dry cat food and water on the back porch. Even though we still could not get close to this cat, he was making himself right at home. Since Toby had not barked at him, I hoped they would get along. But then, Toby was not a big barker.

Later that day, I let Toby out the front door to do his business. He went around the side of the house and was back in a few minutes. I really did not give it much thought until later that evening when Red, as Lucas was now calling the cat, never showed up to eat his dinner. The only thing I knew about cats was that they could be pretty darn independent. So, I was not overly concerned until he did not show up for three days in a row.

On the fourth day, I was doing something on the back porch, when I heard a faint meow.

"Red," I called.

I heard it again. Toby was next to me and he started wagging his tail. Not exactly sure where the noise was coming from, I started walking into the woods behind the house. I heard it again. I started following the sound. The whole time, Toby was beside me with his tail wagging, seeming very excited. By then, I started to get suspicious of Toby and asked, "Toby, where is Red?"

With that, Toby ran to a specific tree, stood at the bottom, and looked up. *Holy Cow!* Red was thirty to forty feet up this pine tree and could not get down. The fact that Toby knew exactly where he was made me believe that Toby had chased him up that tree a few days ago. I went to find Lucas.

"Lucas, look," I said. "That cat has obviously been up there for four days with no food or water. How long can he last?"

"I don't know," Lucas said, nonchalantly.

"Lucas, we have to get him down," I said, somewhat urgently. I was very worried about this poor guy.

If it were up to Lucas, he would have left the cat there to figure it out, but by this time, he had realized it was far easier to appease me than to argue his point. After pondering it for a moment, Lucas offered, "I guess I could cut down the tree."

It was a huge pine tree at the edge of our property.

"Okay," I agreed.

Lucas went to get the chainsaw, as I put Toby back in the house. I was not sure how this was going to work. Red was so high up in the tree, I didn't know what was going to happen to him when it fell. However, we did not seem to have any other options. If I could have called the fire department, I would have, but there was no way they were getting a ladder truck back in those woods. There were still a ton of big branches on this tree, so getting an extension ladder up there would not work either.

Lucas showed up with the chain saw and did not hesitate to get to work. He seemed a little more confident than me that this would work out. Once he started, it took about twenty seconds for the tree to fall over. The large branches seemed to cushion the fall, and once the tree hit the ground, the cat jumped to the ground and took off at a sprint down the driveway.

"Well, I guess he is okay," I said, relieved.

Toby chased Red up a tree three more times. The second time, Lucas got a ladder and was able to reach him, but in doing so, the ladder almost fell over, toppling down a steep hill. The third time, I was able to get on a ladder and reach him. The fourth time, he went even higher up than he did the first time. Lucas refused to cut down another tree, saying that the cat was either going to learn how to get himself down, or he would die up there, and he had never seen a cat skeleton in a tree.

I was not so sure Red would be able to get down. After four days up in that tree, I spent forty-five minutes coaxing him down with a bowl of whipped cream. Once he got about ten feet off the ground, he lost his footing and fell. I managed to catch him. Since then, I began bringing Red inside the house when Lucas was not around to try to get Red and Toby comfortable with each other. It seemed to work.

11

Winter in North Idaho

In the Washington, D. C. area, if we got an inch of snow, everything, including the federal government, seemed to shut down. Having spent our entire lives there, our first few winters here were eye-opening, to say the least. It started snowing in November, and by Thanksgiving, snow was on the ground to stay for the rest of the winter. It seemed to snow every day those first few winters. It was beautiful and a much dryer snow than we were used to. As a result, the roads rarely got slippery. In addition, the county did a good job at keeping the roads plowed. Consequently, schools or businesses hardly ever closed for snow. The people here were used to it and seemed to know how to drive in it.

The only time the conditions ever got icy in Bonners Ferry was if the temperatures warmed during the day, things started to melt and then froze again at night. This did happen on occasion.

One particular winter morning, Lucas was up early, preparing to plow the several inches of snow we had gotten overnight. He did this every morning we had new snow, so I could get to work. The front of our driveway was still terribly steep with a drop-off on one side, and the last thirty feet going up to our house was also relatively steep. As I was eating my cereal and watching out the window, Lucas backed his car out of the driveway and started on his way down to the pole barn to get the tractor. His car seemed to be fishtailing and sliding down that first hill. I stood up to continue watching this and saw him slide directly into the snow berm at the end of that hill. I was thankful that the berm was large enough to stop him from going over the edge and down into the gorge. I wondered just how slippery it was. He could not seem to turn the car to continue down the driveway. After several attempts, Lucas got out of the car, throwing his hands up in the air. I supposed he was planning on walking the rest of the way down when his feet flew right out from under him, and he slid on his butt down the rest of the driveway.

"That is one way to get down there," I muttered to the dog while smiling.

A few minutes later, Lucas came walking into the house.

"Abby, you are not going to work today. There is no way you are getting out of here. The driveway is a three-inch-thick piece of solid ice."

"Okay. Let's give it an hour or two and see how it looks." I had a time-sensitive project I was working on and really needed to get to the office and finish it.

Lucas just shook his head.

Around 11 that morning, it seemed to have warmed up a little, and I was sure the main roads were fine by now. I could use our back driveway, which was not as steep, to get out and I believed I would be fine getting to work. We did not normally use that part of the driveway out of courtesy because it goes right through the neighbor's property. Lucas agreed that the back way would be better if I absolutely had to go to work.

Getting out of the driveway was slow since it was still slick, but I managed. Once on the road, I started down the hill and quickly realized that our road was in no better condition than our front driveway since it was all shaded. I started sliding, and as I struggled to keep the car straight on the road, the back end swung around. I was now going sideways down the hill. Desperately trying to get the car under control, I managed to get a little traction on a bare spot and was able to semi-straighten the car out, but then I was on ice again. All of this seemed to be happening in slow motion.

Next, I was sliding head-on to the edge of the road and a twenty-foot drop down to a creek. There was nothing I could do. I was sliding and heading straight over the side. As I closed my eyes, not wanting to see what was coming, my car jolted to a stop in a huge pile of plowed snow on the side of the road. The car was at a funny angle, but I had, luckily, not gone down that embankment. I opened my door to get out and froze with fear. My car was facing down the embankment while teetering on a snow berm. The rear wheels of my Rav4 were off of the ground, and the front wheels were airborne on the other side of the berm. *Holy Cow!* Realizing that any sudden movement could send the entire car down that embankment, I froze, afraid to breathe. I slowly reached over, grabbed my phone off the front passenger seat, and carefully started to contemplate my next move. I decided it would be best to jump out of this car as quickly as I could. I needed to get out of the way in case it fell down the hill toward the stream. I took a deep breath, counted to three, and half jumped and half hurled myself out of the car, falling into the snow pile and rolling as quickly and as far away from that car as I could. In a panic, I called Lucas, who said he would be right there.

Lucas arrived a few minutes later, with chains on his tractor. After spending a minute looking at our new predicament, he questioned, "Damn, Abby. How in the world did that happen?"

"I'm not exactly sure. But, I am so relieved I didn't go down the embankment and into the creek."

He was hoping he could pull me out. However, given the fact that none of my wheels were currently on solid ground, we both questioned whether that was even possible. Lucas hooked a chain up to my car and tried and tried, but there was too much ice. The tractor had no traction, even with chains on the wheels.

We called for a tow truck and waited for forty-five minutes, absolutely freezing on the side of the road.

"I sure hope that is not the tow truck," I said, as I pointed to a truck sliding sideways down the hill toward us.

"It is," Lucas said with heightened concern in his voice. "Abby, get off the road."

After slipping and sliding, Lucas and I both made it off the side of the road and crawled up on an embankment. Thankfully, the tow truck stopped without crashing into us. The tow truck hooked up to my car and tried to winch it out, which only resulted in the tow truck being pulled closer to my car and the drop-off. There was just too much ice on the road, and even the tow truck had no traction.

Eventually, Lucas and the tow truck driver had the idea to tie the tow truck to a tree across the road with heavy chains and then try to pull me out. That worked, and they managed to pull my car out. After thanking the driver profusely and paying him, I got back in my Rav4, cranked up the heat, and crept up our back driveway to the house. It turned out I would not be going to work after all. There were not too many days where I could not make it to work, but this was one of them.

• • • ● • ● • • •

A few weeks later, we had gotten about two and a half feet of heavy wet snow overnight. In addition, the high winds created three-to-four-foot drifts. Lucas said it would take him a while to plow the driveway. Since he never says that, I started to worry about feeding the horses, who were half-way down the driveway. They are used to eating at 7:30 every morning. I knew the importance of having horses on a schedule to avoid ailments like colic. Lucas always started plowing at the bottom of the driveway where we kept the tractor and worked his way up. I watched him start to hike down there in hip-deep snow, which looked like a ton of work. I was not doing that.

I decided to get the snow shovel and make a path down to the barn, determined to get to the horses and feed them before mid-afternoon. I knew it was a long way, and this was heavy, wet snow, but it was best to keep the horses as close to a normal schedule as possible. I started shoveling a path along the side of the driveway. It was slow-going, but I persisted, throwing huge shovels full of snow off to the side. I was absolutely getting my workout in and was positive I would feel it later that night. There is no need for a gym membership when living on a farm, that is for sure. There always seemed to be something physical to keep us in shape.

It took me about forty-five minutes to get within fifteen feet of the barn, when up the driveway came Lucas. He continued plowing right by me, as he smiled and waved. In less than five minutes, he had plowed up to our house. I stood there watching him get closer to the house feeling a combination of stunned and peeved. Peeved, because he saw me starting to shovel a path and never said a word. I just spent forty-five minutes shoveling because he said it would take him a while to plow the driveway. Apparently, our ideas of "a while" were vastly different.

· · · ●·●·● · ● · ·

Later that week, after even more snowfall, Lucas went out to plow the driveway early in the morning. He was back within a few minutes.

"Abby, I need your help. I got the tractor stuck in the ditch on the side of the driveway. I need you to pull me out with the plow truck."

"Really? Okay, how do I do that?"

"I'll help you. Bring the plow truck down to me," Lucas said as he started walking back down the driveway.

I had never driven the old plow truck and hoped I remembered how to drive a stick shift. My very first car, a Honda Accord, had been a stick shift. I hadn't driven a manual car since I sold it—in my early twenties. Lucas walked over and showed me how to raise and lower the plow. There were a lot of levers and things to remember.

I put it in gear as Lucas continued walking. Once we reached the tractor, Lucas hooked up the chains and directed me to back up slowly. We pulled the tractor out in no time. He unhooked the chains and told me to continue down the driveway until I could easily turn around.

Once I turned around, I thought it would be a good idea to raise the plow a little since I would now be going uphill. Lucas had done an exceptionally nice job of plowing this part of the driveway, so I wasn't too worried. I fiddled with the plow lever, and it seemed it wouldn't go any higher, or so I thought. I played with a few of the other levers and couldn't really tell that they did much of anything. *Oh well! I'm probably fine.*

I continued up the hill, and as I got within sight of Lucas, he started yelling and waving his arms frantically. I couldn't make out what he was saying, nor could I see well over the front of the truck because of the steep incline, so I waited until I got a little closer to stop. Whatever he was saying, he sounded exasperated and seemed like he was about to blow a gasket.

"What?" I hollered back as I rolled down my window.

Lucas walked over to the truck, leaned into my window, and said in a calm voice, "Do you realize you have the plow down and angled so you are now pushing all of the snow back into the driveway?"

"No. Actually, I can't see well over the front of the truck because of the incline. Huh. I guess that's why it seemed to be getting harder and harder to drive up the hill. Oops! I'm sorry." I guess those levers did something after all.

Without another word, Lucas reached inside the truck and put the plow up.

"Go ahead and take it back to the pole barn," he said calmly as he backed up and directed me around my new pile of snow. He shook his head as he walked back to the tractor, getting ready to plow the lower part of the driveway again.

I knew I was lucky that Lucas had such a calm demeanor when dealing with me. Some husbands and wives would've had big fights over something like this. Lucas always seemed to be very forgiving when it came to me, even when I didn't feel I deserved it.

• • • • ● • ● • • • •

Over those first few winters, while I was busy working, Lucas looked for things to get into, which resulted in several fiascos of sorts. Between those fiascos and the looming north Idaho winter weather we were facing, we were in for a very eventful winter. Lucas, wanting to take full advantage of living here, decided we had to have snowmobiles. I thought that would be fun and envisioned riding them around our seventy-acre field. Lucas had completely different ideas.

After purchasing our first two snowmobiles, we spent the weekend getting familiar with them and riding them around our mostly flat field in about two feet of snow. The sleds were much larger than I imagined and a little harder to control than I expected. I had no idea they could reach speeds of one hundred mph or more. I struggled to keep control at twenty to twenty-five mph. Lucas had no problem flying by me. I managed for about thirty minutes. After thirty minutes of snow flying back in my face, even with goggles, and blanketing me in enough snow that I resembled a snowman, I was freezing. I needed to remember to dress warmer the next time.

A few days later, Lucas suggested we take the snowmobiles up Hall Mountain. He had spoken to a few of the guys in the neighborhood, Kenny and Chase, who spent a lot of time in the winter snowmobiling in the surrounding mountains. They offered to take us with them any time we wanted. They were brothers and roughly twenty years younger than us. Their family moved here from Spokane, Washington, when Kenny was three years old. Chase was born here the following year. They shared a property on our road, Kenny in a house and Chase in a newer single-wide trailer. They grew up in these mountains, hunting, hiking, and skiing. However, they lived to snowmobile in the winters, always willing to take new snowmobilers with them. Lucas spoke with them again and found out we needed a few other pieces of gear before going. Lucas said he would take care of it. We made plans to go with them the following weekend. I didn't really give it much more thought.

That Wednesday, when I got home from work, Lucas told me he had taken care of purchasing everything we needed to go snowmobiling in the mountains.

"Great," I said. "Let me see it."

We walked into the guest bedroom where he had everything laid out on the bed. *Holy Cow!* There was a ton of stuff there. He had purchased one-piece snowmobile suits for each of us, heavy-duty helmets, heated gloves, and snowmobile boots. I had no idea there were boots and snowsuits specifically engineered for this. In addition, there were folding shovels, walkie-talkies, and something else.

"First of all, why do we need those big helmets? I thought we were just going to be riding on logging roads," I asked.

"Abby, they are just for added protection."

"What are these?" I asked, referring to two pouches with antennae.

"Those are avalanche packs and beacons. One for each of us."

"What? We need those, why? Aren't we just staying on the logging roads?" I was starting to get more than a little worried. I looked at Lucas with an expression of growing doubt.

"Yes. At least most of the time. These are just a precaution. The avalanche packs will act like an airbag if we are caught in an avalanche, helping to keep us toward the top of the snow and hopefully allowing us to breathe until help arrives. The shovels are in case we need to dig out from anywhere. The avalanche beacons are so we can locate each other if one of us gets lost in an avalanche. But, we will be fine. It cannot be that hard. Don't worry."

"Right."

I had to hand it to him. He certainly seemed to have thought of everything. From the looks of things, I was sure we were going to be warm if nothing else. I was starting to get concerned, nonetheless.

"And, what are those two little metal boxes for?" I asked, picking up one.

"We put smokies in those and attach them to our exhaust pipe, which warms them up while we are riding. They will be our lunch when we get where we are going," Lucas explained.

Great. Nothing like a little exhaust fume-tasting smokies to look forward to.

· · · · · · · · · · ·

When that day finally arrived, I was getting cold feet before we even left, suggesting Lucas go without me. I even briefly thought about faking a cold. Lucas assured me we would be fine. We packed everything up and put the sleds on the trailer. We drove to the bottom of our driveway, where Kenny and Chase were waiting for us in their truck. We pulled out behind them and followed them to our new adventure.

About an hour later, after winding up sketchy snow and ice-covered mountain roads, we arrived at our parking spot. We took the sleds off the trailer and spent a good thirty minutes putting on the snowsuit, helmet, snowmobile boots, avalanche pack, beacon, and walkie-talkies. The helmet alone weighed at least ten pounds. I felt like I was ready for a space mission, not to mention gaining about twenty-five pounds. Chase did a quick run-through of what happens if any of us gets caught in an avalanche and what we should do. The sheer fact that he felt it necessary to go over all of that made me queasy.

By then, I had a fair amount of anxiety and trepidation; I would have much rather been under a blanket on my couch with my dog next to me, reading a book. *Why did I agree to do this? Lucas gets me into the worst situations at times.*

"We are going to continue following the logging road for a few more miles up the mountain before getting off the road," says Kenny.

I give Lucas an alarming look. "I thought we were staying on the road?"

He, again, tried to reassure me that we would be fine. "It will be just like in our field."

Right. Here we go.

As we started up the road, Kenny was leading, with Chase, Lucas, and then me. Being in the back, I was having a hard time keeping up with everyone. *They are going a lot faster than me—too fast.* I was still worried about the icy parts. Eventually, Lucas noticed me falling behind a little, and he got behind me. Thankful for that, we continued. After about thirty minutes, the road started getting narrower. The left side of that road was now a sheer cliff that dropped down a good thirty feet or more. The snow was getting deeper and on our right was a steep wall. Our margin for error was becoming increasingly smaller, and I was becoming more nervous. I had a death grip on the handlebars, my heart was racing, and I was nauseous. Kenny and Chase did not appear phased by any of these things, and they never seemed to slow down. I was not comfortable at all. We eventually reached the part where we got off the road and stopped for lunch. Prying my fingers off the handlebars, I was so relieved to be stopped.

By then, I had to pee badly and could not wait for this day to be over. I saw a strand of pine trees not too far away that looked like a good place to go. I stood up, stepped off my sled, and sank in powder up to my waist.

"Ahhh," I scream. "I can't move!"

"Abby, what are you doing?" I heard Lucas say.

"I have to get over there to pee."

"Just try taking small steps and packing the snow under each step until you get there," offered Kenny.

I tried and I tried and I tried, not getting anywhere fast. All the gear designed to save me was going to kill me while trying to pee. It was going to take me all day just to get back on my sled, and I had to get to those pine trees first. I spent the next half an hour stepping, crawling, climbing, shimmying, rolling, and pushing snow, trying to get to those pine trees any way I could, while the boys seemed to be having fun, playing in the snow with the snowmobiles and not paying any attention to me, whatsoever. *Why in the world did I agree to do this? This is not fun, and it is cold.* By the time I reached the pine trees, I was about as exhausted as I had ever been in my life. The way back was not as bad, since I had already worn a path of sorts. It still was not easy.

Once I got back to my sled and managed to awkwardly pull myself up and on it, I got a better look at where exactly we were. This was not a flat field like I had envisioned or like Lucas had indicated. It was the side of a mountain with various vertical grades. Nothing there was even close to flat. After we ate, I watched Kenny and Chase ride all over that mountainside, crashing into trees on several occasions and almost rolling their sleds while side-hilling at other times. They seemed to be having a ball. I was not feeling it. Lucas was a little more reserved yet still doing way more than I was comfortable with. I happily sat there on my sled and watched, quietly praying that there would be no avalanche and we would all get out of there unharmed.

"Abby, come on. This is fun," Lucas said as he pulled up beside me.

"I am having fun just watching. Thanks. It is so beautiful up here." Trying to sound as positive as I could, not wanting to put a damper on their fun. However, I was exhausted from my trek to the pine trees.

"I will just sit here and finish eating my exhaust-flavored smokie," I mumbled to myself.

It really was gorgeous. All the branches on the pine trees were heavy with snow, and the ground was covered with virgin, crisp, clear white snow. It looked like something out of a National Geographic Magazine. The only way to get there and see that was by snowmobile. Because of that, I felt privileged.

After about an hour, we all started back down the mountain. I was happy to be heading home and was sure we would all sleep well that night. This time, Lucas was in front, and I was right behind him. Kenny and Chase were in the back. At one point, we all stopped, and as Lucas stood up on his sled and turned around to holler something at all of us, he inadvertently hit his throttle with his knee and his sled went flying off the cliff, airborne, with him on it.

There was about a forty-foot drop that was ten or fifteen feet wide. He cleared the gulch, hitting the tops of the pine trees. The impact stopped his sled, but Lucas went flying over the pine trees, head first, to the other side of the gulch. That may have been the most terrifying moment of my life.

"Oh My God!" I screamed.

I turned off my sled, jumped off, and was now hysterical.

"Oh My God, he went all the way over those trees. Is there any way he is going to be alive?"

I was crying now and screaming for Lucas, when Chase grabbed my arm and said, "Wait. Listen."

I stop crying for a second.

"I am okay. I'm okay—just stuck," came a voice from across that gulch.

Holy cow! Could he really be okay?

"Lucas," I yelled again, "Are you sure you're okay?"

"Yes. I landed in deep snow. I have no idea how I am going to get back there though."

At that moment, I noticed how far down his snowmobile had fallen into the gulch after hitting the tree tops. Even though Lucas seemed to be okay, the severity of the situation was just setting in.

How in the world were we going to get Lucas and his snowmobile back up on this road? Even if, by some miracle, we did that, I was sure the snowmobile was totaled. *How are we going to get out of these mountains? The whole day was a terrible idea. Lucas and I have no business doing this in these mountains. It was only the second time we have been on snowmobiles. He should have known better. I should have listened to my gut.*

Kenny and Chase were already in motion. They were unpacking a come-along and rope, and Chase was starting down the side of the cliff we were on with his backpack. Kenny was following while hollering to Lucas to try to make it to the bottom of the gulch by his sled, and they would meet him there. He told him to keep talking until they could see each other so he could find his way. They told me to stay with the sleds in case we needed to send a distress signal. *A distress signal!*

I felt so utterly helpless, at this point. I did not have the shear strength this was going to require to do anything other than what I was doing, which was nothing, just sitting there with the sleds. Thank God these two guys were younger, in good shape, and with us. I could not seem to stop crying and cussing Lucas out under my breath. This had been one of his worsts ideas yet.

Lucas made it to the bottom seemingly unscathed. It took another four and a half long hours to pull that snowmobile up from the gulch, inch by inch. I was so relieved that Lucas was okay and beyond surprised when they got his snowmobile running. I began crying again—tears of relief. The rest of the ride down that mountain was a blur. We made it back to our trucks with about five minutes of daylight left. It had been one long, terrible day.

Once we got back into the truck and it was just Lucas and I, my anger at that entire idea started surfacing.

"Lucas, seriously?" I started yelling. "Did you have any idea what that was going to be like? You, we, could have been killed out there today. When they told you we needed avalanche packs and beacons and collapsing shovels, did that not give you any clue? Where is your common sense?"

"Abby, it was not that bad. We are all okay, and besides, we made a memory," Lucas said very calmly, trying to defuse the situation.

"Right. We are so very lucky."

We did not speak the rest of the way home. Later that night, as Lucas was getting ready to take a shower, I noticed black and purple bruises on his arm and the side of his ribs. He noticed it at the same moment, in the mirror.

"Ouch," he muttered.

"Wow. I am just so glad you are okay," I said, still not sure if I wanted to hug him or hit him, at that moment.

As we were falling asleep in bed that night, I said, "It really was beautiful up there. However, from now on, I will stick to snowmobiling around our house."

Lucas went up in those mountains a few more times with the neighbors and always managed to come home with bruises and sore muscles, yet always in one piece. I don't think any of those subsequent trips in the mountains were as eventful as that first time. Every time he went, I worried until he got back home. He eventually decided he could not keep up with the younger guys anymore. Thank goodness.

Winters are not for the weak, in strength or mind, in north Idaho.

· · · ● · ● · · · ·

Later that winter, Lucas had to fly back to Virginia for a family emergency. He was there for ten days. While he was gone, I was completely alone on our property at the very end of a county road. My parents, who by then were living in another house on our property, were also in Virginia, visiting my brother. Our property is extremely remote with no visible neighbors or anyone within shouting distance. I had to stay behind to take care of the horses, chickens, dog, and cat. The downside to living with livestock in the winter is, it is very hard to find someone to take care of your animals at a moment's notice. This is especially true when you factor in that our driveway is almost a mile long and would need to be plowed if it snowed, which it does frequently in the winter here, to get to our animals to feed them.

It just so happened that they were forecasting a huge snowstorm two days after he left. They were calling for up to three feet of snow, more in the higher elevations. In addition, the temperature was forecasted to hover between minus ten and five for four days in a row. That normally does not happen. I was well prepared, though. I had plenty of food. If the power went out, which it sometimes does with heavy snowfalls, I had plenty of wood for the woodstove. The only thing I had to worry about was getting back and forth to the barn to feed the horses every day. The barn was about a half-mile down the driveway from our house. I was sure I could figure that out. I felt prepared for whatever was to come my way.

· · · ● · ● · ● · ·

I woke up that morning with a strange feeling of being watched. As I rolled over in bed and looked out the window, there was Red, sitting on top of the hot tub, just outside our bedroom window, staring at me again. When we adopted him, or should I say when he adopted us, he was supposed to be a barn cat and catch mice. Once I started feeding him on the covered back porch, he rarely left it. Since Lucas had been gone, Red had been doing this every morning. I'd wake up, and he would be staring at me from the top of the hot tub. I figured it might have something to do with the hot tub cover being slightly warmer than anywhere else on the patio. He had recently taken a liking to Lucas and would follow him around outside. Neither Lucas nor I had ever owned a cat or particularly wanted one. While Red had worked his way into our hearts and family in the short time since he had arrived, Toby was still not so sure about him. I hoped they would eventually accept each other.

· · · ● · ● · ● · ·

Overnight, we had gotten just shy of the three feet of snow they had been forecasting. It was still coming down, and it was a whopping four degrees. I had never actually plowed the driveway but had seen Lucas do it plenty of times. Lucas never wanted me to do it. To get to the horses, however, I would need to. Otherwise, walking in hip-deep snow back and forth every day would get exhausting. Besides, Lucas always liked to remind me that I could not survive here without him. I disagreed. This was a chance to prove to him what I was capable of.

After a quick breakfast and feeding the dog and cat, I spent twenty minutes bundling up and then walked down to the tractor inside our pole barn. I climbed up and turned the key to start it. It made a slight turnover noise and then nothing. I tried again. It barely turned over. I tried a few more times until nothing happened. I must have killed it. The tractor was dead. I told myself it was probably too cold for it, anyway. *Well crap! Now what?*

I quickly remembered our 1972 plow truck, which was our backup. It was down near the horse barn, and it could be temperamental. I believe it was usually hooked up to a battery charger since I had heard Lucas talk about that. *If I could get down there, maybe I could figure that out.* Trudging through three feet of snow was not as bad as I initially expected since it was dry fluffy snow.

Once there, I opened the hood of the truck and stood there, trying to figure out what the heck was going on. It looked like there were two batteries connected with jumper cables. There was an extension cord connected to something else. I wondered if there was a specific order I needed to unhook everything in, so I wouldn't blow anything up. *This is what it must feel like to work on a bomb squad, sweating it out while guessing whether to cut the green wire or the yellow one. Where should I begin?*

I didn't ponder this too long, as my hands were freezing. I just unhooked things, one at a time, and was grateful nothing blew up in the process. I closed the hood, climbed inside, and slightly turned the key in the ignition. I hesitated for a second, pressed the clutch and brake, and turned the key the whole way. The truck started right up. There was no real heat in the truck, so I needed to work quickly.

After fumbling for a few minutes with what buttons and levers did what, I had only driven this truck one other time, and that hadn't gone well, I put the truck into first gear and slowly moved forward a few feet. *So far, so good.* I stopped at the end of the building and put the plow down, moving forward again, I pushed some snow up against a tree. It was working, and I was feeling good about it. Lucas should know better than to doubt me. I backed up a little, turned the wheel, and continued straight up the driveway. I kept having to stop every fifteen or twenty yards and push the snow off the side. There was a lot of snow. I was also trying to be extra careful not to plow all the gravel off the driveway in the process. Lucas would have a cow if I did that. I was getting more and more confident the further up the driveway I got.

I made it up to the part of our driveway just before we have to turn to go up to our house, about twenty yards from the house. I had to make a hard right turn and did not quite make it all the way. I stopped, put the truck into reverse, and backed up a little to correct this. I must have misjudged how far the top of the ravine was on the other side of the driveway behind me. It was hard to see with so much snow. The defroster wasn't working, and the windows were completely fogged. I seemed to have gotten stuck. After getting out to check, it appeared I had one rear wheel completely hanging over the side. While I felt in no danger of going over the edge, I was not getting that truck unstuck anytime soon.

Well, shoot! To make matters worse, the truck was now positioned horizontally across the width of the driveway, completely blocking anyone from getting to our house, assuming the rest of the driveway would be miraculously plowed soon. On the positive side, at least I could walk back and forth daily to feed our horses. I walked back down to the barn and fed and watered the horses, who were acting like they hadn't been fed in a month. They were so used to eating at 7:30 on the dot, and it was getting close to 9:00. I then headed back to the house.

The tractor was dead, and the plow truck was out of commission. I hoped that we would not get any more snow before Lucas got home. In addition, the ridiculously frigid temperatures were making Copper's sheath swell and I had to massage it three or four times every day to keep the blood flowing.

That evening, just before dark, I looked out the front window and noticed there was a small herd of elk in the middle of our snow-covered field. With the snow-covered mountains in the background, I thought, as I had so many times, how lucky we were to live in such a beautiful place.

Lucas called later that evening to check in, and I told him everything was fine. I had no intention of saying otherwise. I certainly was not going to mention the tractor and plow truck.

The next morning, as it was just beginning to get light outside, I noticed the elk were still out front. However, they had moved across the field, found their way into our pole barn, and were happily munching away on our large round bales of hay. That hay was for our horses and we only had so many bales to last the winter. I had to do something.

I put on my coveralls, snow gear, and heated gloves. It was still hovering around zero degrees. I walked down there, yelling at them to get away. They did not seem phased. I got within fifteen feet of them. They were much larger up close. I waved my arms and yelled. A few of them paused from eating, looked at me, then went right back to eating. They were not backing down. I suppose, with all the snow we had recently gotten, that food was a little hard for them to find. This was too good of a food source for them to give up so easily.

I walked back up to the house, thinking that I would get Lucas's new truck since it was bigger than my Rav4 and probably safer in the snow and drive down there to scare those elk. I got the keys to Lucas's new truck, which was in the garage, and thought for a minute. *Maybe, if I drive down there, beep the horn, yell, AND shoot Lucas's pistol up in the air—that would surely scare them off.* I went back into the house and grabbed Lucas's revolver out of his nightstand. Up until that point, I had been adamant about not wanting anything to do with a gun.

When home alone, I preferred to sleep with a hammer under my pillow. The first time Lucas went to Virginia and I was alone, the Schwann man had come by my office and done his best to convince us he saw a Yeti in his backyard. He said he even had him on camera. I thought he was a little out of his mind, not believing in such things. However, that night, the wind blew harder than normal. It blew so hard that it moved the deck furniture around outside of my bedroom window, and I started to wonder if just maybe it was possible. In addition, Lucas didn't believe in drapes or blinds in any of the windows since no one was supposed to be around our house. The only sort of weapon I could find quickly was a screwdriver.

That would work. I put it under my pillow. Since I am such a sound sleeper, likely I wouldn't know there was an intruder in the house until they were literally on top of me. At that point, it would be easy to grab my screwdriver and stick it in their eye. At least, that is what I believed.

It wasn't until Lucas came home and found that screwdriver under his pillow and sheets and towels tacked to the walls in front of the windows, that we had that discussion. He wanted me to learn how to use a gun and keep it next to the bed. I refused. We compromised, and I agreed to use a hammer instead of a screwdriver. Lucas thought I had a better fighting chance with that. He also agreed to put blinds in our bedroom and bathroom windows.

As I was backing the truck out of the garage, which in my defense was a tight fit, I heard and felt a crack and thud. *Oh crap!* I had just busted Lucas's passenger side mirror. Lucas was going to kill me. I continued toward those stubborn elk, who were starting to pay attention to me, as I honked the horn. Still, they were not moving from their spot. I rolled down my window and was honking the horn, yelling, and now shooting Lucas's gun up in the air. That finally did it. I got their attention, and the entire herd turned and went running into the woods. I had done it. They were gone for now. I just needed to make sure they could not get back into that hay.

I looked around the pole barn for ideas on how to do this and decided to barricade the hay as much as possible. I needed to keep that hay safe, at least until Lucas got home. I stacked some pallets around the bottom of the bales, leaned our kayaks and canoe up against other bales, put a tarp across some of them, and wrapped a rope around all of this to keep things in place. I leaned some fencing panels and anything else I could find, over the rest of it. I was not sure if this would be enough to keep the elk out, but it was enough of a mess that it would probably scare them away. I had no idea what else to do.

I drove back up to the house. I now had to figure out what to do about Lucas's side mirror on his truck. He just bought the truck a month ago. It was brand new. I felt terrible. The mirror was shattered, but the rest of it was not too bad. I had a travel make-up mirror about the same size as that mirror. Maybe I could substitute it and he would not even notice. I took a photo of it first and, for some reason, thought I'd use my network of friends on Facebook for ideas on how to do that. I really needed to fix it before Lucas got home. Lucas only goes on Facebook early in the morning. He has always been a man of routines, never wavering far from them. I would make sure to delete this entire post before then. I quickly received a whole bunch of ideas. I was starting to feel hopeful that I could fix this. Then, one friend messaged, "Aren't you afraid of your husband seeing this post?"

"No. He only checks Facebook in the morning."

The very next post, "Too late. Husband has already seen this." It was Lucas.

Well, crap. What are the chances of that happening? I fixed it as best as I could and even used white duct tape to match the white paint on the truck. Lucas was not amused but brushed it off as an accident, which it was. There were times when his laid-back demeanor was a blessing. This was one of those times.

• • • ● • ● • ● • • •

Three days later, Lucas was on his way home from the Spokane airport, thank God. Once the county finally plowed our road, I had gotten a neighbor to plow our driveway up to where the plow truck was stuck. At least it was something. Lucas still did not know about any of this.

I was in the kitchen when he came walking through the door with his suitcase. It was just starting to get dark outside.

"Hi," I said.

"Hello. Abby, why is the plow truck across the driveway?" Lucas said with a very puzzled look on his face, almost like he really didn't want to know the answer.

"Why don't you unpack first and then open a beer."

"Abby, do I need a beer?"

"Maybe a couple. I already have them in the fridge for you," I replied, trying my best to smile.

"Okay. This should be good," I heard him utter under his breath, as he walked into the bedroom.

When he was done unpacking, Lucas finally grabbed his beer, and we sat down. I told him everything. The entire time, he never said a word. He just kept looking at me with a questioning look. When I was done, he asked if I remembered about the glow plugs on the tractor? I told him I had not. He just shook his head. I sat there silently, waiting for him to say something, for the longest minute.

"So," Lucas began, "what I have learned from this is, it is way more expensive to go away and leave you home alone."

Then he started to laugh. I asked him what was so funny.

"The image of you driving my truck, laying on the horn, screaming at the elk, while shooting my gun up in the air. I wish I could have seen that."

"Hey. It worked. I would say I managed just fine," I said with a smile. "Although I am very glad to have you back home.

As I was falling asleep, I thought Lucas sure seemed to take everything well. *I hope he is in just as good of a mood when he sees the mess in the pole barn in the morning.*

• • • ●•● ● • • •

The next morning, Lucas nudged me awake.

"Abby, what is Red doing? He has been sitting there, staring at us for the last twenty minutes."

"Oh, Red. He has been doing that every morning. I wake up and he is sitting there staring at me."

"Very odd," Lucas mumbled.

12

Getting Back into Real Estate

By late winter, early spring, after working for a local real estate company for several months, I started to get busier. I really enjoyed selling real estate and was much more comfortable than I had been as the 4-H coordinator. If working for 4-H had allowed me to meet most of the people in the county, working in real estate in north Idaho allowed me to see some beautiful and surprising properties as well as some truly shocking places.

Many of the properties I showed to clients were bare, remote pieces of land. There was a safety issue for me when showing random clients these properties. First, it was not completely safe for me to take strangers to these properties by myself. Fortunately, since Lucas was retired, he and Toby could usually accompany me on these showings. When they were not able to go with me, I had a handful of friends who were retired law enforcement, and I could count on at least one of them to go. Second, when showing these properties, I would need to have some sort of protection. It was not only the people I needed to be wary of; the wildlife was also a significant factor. We had everything from mountain lions, coyotes, black bears, grizzlies, elk, moose, and deer to wolves. I had even heard of one instance where friends of ours ran into a wolverine while riding their horses, and it chased them.

Lucas finally convinced me that I should carry a concealed gun when showing these properties. I would need to learn how to use it first. Let me just say, there are some things a husband and wife should not do together. Teaching me how to use a gun was one of them. Lucas had a small arsenal of guns. One of his side jobs in Virginia, after retiring and before moving here, was a tactical gun instructor for the NRA. He knew what he was doing. We decided that the easiest gun from his arsenal for me to manage was a 38-revolver. After shooting his shotgun from his porch years ago, I wanted something that did not have too much kickback. I did not like the 9mm he had offered me.

We set up targets outside, and Lucas tried to help me, which resulted in him losing patience and tears on my part. I just could not hit the middle of the target no matter what he said or how hard I tried. He did not know what else to do. We agreed that I would find somebody else to teach me.

We had friends who were retired law enforcement from California, Amy and Sean. Sean had built a shooting range in their basement, and he agreed to help me. We spent several days in that shooting range, learning how to draw and shoot from a concealed position. We shot and shot until my fingers were blistered. I still had a hard time hitting the target. I would line up the gun and look past the site at the target every time, but it just would not work. Finally, Sean said, the site should be clear and the target blurry. Ahh . . . it dawned on me that I needed my reading glasses for that to work. I put them on, and bam, I hit the bull's eye. I did it several more times in a row. I was so excited. I was doing it. But, wait.

"If I am ever in a position, where I need to draw my gun and shoot quickly, I won't have time to put my reading glasses on," I said.

"That's okay," Sean explained. "If you are ever in that situation, you can at least get the bullet within a close enough area. And, Abby, if you ever are in that situation, you will probably be within ten feet of the person, and remember to shoot to kill, not injure. Just don't shoot them in the back, because then we will really have a problem."

Sean also gave me numerous other tips, like never walking in front of somebody. Always let them walk in front of me and never let them know I am carrying. My favorite tip was, "What do ya do, if you are coming out of a store at night and your car is in the back of the parking lot and some guy is hanging around it?"

"I wait to walk to my car until he is no longer there, or, have someone walk me to it," I replied confidently.

"Nah," Sean snapped. "Do you have a high-powered flashlight, like this one?" Sean held up a tactical-looking flashlight.

"Yes, I do." I had, in fact, recently purchased one for when I took the dog out at night.

"Well, keep it in your purse. If you need to walk to your car in the dark at night and someone is hanging around your car, you take that flashlight in one hand and gun in the other." Sean was demonstrating how you put one hand over the other while shining the light right at the guy's face. "Then you say, loudly and forcefully, 'BACK AWAY FROM THE CAR! BACK AWAY FROM THE CAR!'"

Oh my gosh, I could just not see myself doing that. The thought of me doing that made me giggle. *I think I will have someone walk me to my car.*

However, I felt comfortable enough with my gun and with my ability to protect myself if needed. Hopefully, that need would never arise. In the meantime, I liked carrying my concealed gun. I felt braver—like I may actually be assimilating to this lifestyle.

• • • • • • • • • •

The very next week, I was in the office when a man named Nico walked in. Nico was a five-foot-two, older Italian gentleman with short gray hair, combed straight back with some sort of gel. He had a very pleasant, laid-back personality. Nico wore jeans, hiking boots, and a beige button-down fishing shirt. He had just retired from Martin Brower, where he had driven a truck for thirty years, supplying food for McDonald's. He was relocating to Bonners Ferry from New Jersey, and his accent reminded me of Joe Pesci in *My Cousin Vinny*. I kept expecting him to say "fa ged about it." Nico wanted to see a piece of property that had an old off-grid house on it and was in a sketchy area. He didn't have much money to spend, so we were limited as to what properties he could consider. I would do my best to find him several things to look at. I told him I would set that particular showing up for the next day, and we agreed to meet back at my office at 9 a.m. Lucas and Toby agreed to come with me.

The next morning Lucas, Toby, and I picked up Nico up in my Rav4. I planned on sitting in the back with Toby, but Nico insisted he sat back there, assuring us how much he liked dogs. We drove down an old, rutty dirt road, which still had areas of melting snow on it since it was mid-spring, for what seemed like an hour before arriving at the property. Once Nico and Lucas realized they were both from New Jersey, they were like two long-lost brothers. They talked for the entire ride, mostly about how much they missed good Italian food. Lucas grew up in a small Italian neighborhood in New Jersey just outside of New York. Once in a while, usually when wine was involved, Lucas slipped back into a little bit of that Jersey Italian accent. He was, whether consciously or unconsciously, completely mimicking Nico's accent. I believed he was totally unaware of it.

The old house was locked. The listing agent told us there was no key and to please not try to get inside the house. It was a safety issue. The house was given no value on this property, and I could see why. It was the size of my garden shed. It appeared to be pieced together with various pieces of scrap plywood and cinder blocks. The metal roof was decent enough looking. Once we stood on the rotting wood steps leading to the front door, we could see through the windows. It wasn't much of a house. It was a one-room cabin of sorts. Inside there was a lot of plywood, no insulation, an old rusty woodstove, and no apparent running water. Nico said not to worry. If he were to purchase the property, he would, "Knock that puppy down and start over."

The rest of the property was in dire need of some cleanup and attention. There was an old ratty-looking gold and brown lazy boy recliner sitting in the mud and various pieces of scrap metal and chicken fencing scattered everywhere. There was an outhouse just inside the trees.

Toby and Lucas were exploring the property, as I was walking it with Nico. I always felt safer having Toby there because if there was any wildlife in the area, he would surely chase them away. As Nico and I were walking back toward the car, I heard a splash. I turned and saw Toby in a hole that was about two and a half feet deep with water. Since Toby is not a water dog and cannot swim, I instinctively ran over to help him, but he quickly figured out how to climb out of there and shook himself off.

"Uh oh," said Nico. "I think dats de old outhouse hole."

"Oh no!"

Upon closer inspection, it absolutely was. Toby now stunk horribly. I didn't have to get too close to him to confirm that. There was no place to clean him off. I did not even have a towel in the car. We had to put him in the car like that and drive the hour back to the office where we had met Nico that morning. On that drive, I insisted I sit in the back with Toby. After that, Nico insisted on following me in his own car whenever we looked at properties, and I always kept an extra towel in the car for Toby.

· · · ● · ● · ● · ·

A few days later, I got a call from a man named Barry who wanted to list his property in Moyie Springs. This would be my first listing. I was so excited. I agreed to meet him on his twenty-acre property. He gave me directions and told me to look for the yurt on the property, which is where he lived. I didn't know what a yurt was, but I was sure I would find it.

Again, I brought Lucas and Toby with me. This property was not much better than the one with the outhouse, just larger and with more junk. It was mostly treed with occasional open spaces that were full of crap. There was an old abandoned school bus sitting in the middle of the property, along with several versions of dilapidated old pole barns, or outbuildings. There was an old bathtub sitting up on cinderblocks with the remnants of a fire underneath it. I wondered if Barry took his baths there? There was an outhouse and numerous clothes lines hanging in the trees. In addition, there was a lot of stuff lying everywhere such as old buckets, rusty oil cans, dirty old mason jars, corroded-looking motors, and a flat-bed trailer.

We found the yurt just as Barry was coming out of it. He was about five feet tall and maybe sixty-five years old. He had long grayish-blond hair in a ponytail. He wore a knitted beanie on his head and carried ski poles when he walked even though the temperature was in the sixties—a quirky little guy, to say the least.

Barry wanted to give us a tour of his property, so we followed. We walked all over that property. He showed us his five-hundred-gallon cement water cistern that he had built. That was his drinking and bathing water. Next to that, was a large, wobbly, wooden structure that he explained was for shaking huckleberries out of their bushes. This required the entire bush to be dug up and put into that contraption. Never mind that it was illegal to uproot a huckleberry bush in that area. They only grow at a specific altitude in the mountains. To my knowledge, no one had ever been successful in growing them commercially there; therefore, they were protected. There were the remnants of two old houses in various stages of deterioration. Neither was salvageable. He showed us what was left of his fenced garden. It was terribly overgrown. I had even walked by it one time without noticing it. There were, however, great views from several spots that would make good building sites for a house once a few trees were cleared. It was a semi-private location. Semi-private because the neighbors' backyards ran along a fence abutting Barry's property. Those houses were visible, even if at a distance. I agreed to list it, not sure if it would ever sell. I was trying to keep an open mind. Boy, was this different from selling real estate in Virginia.

Since Barry did not have any internet or cell phone service, he had initially called me from his friend's cell phone. The only way I could communicate with him was by physically driving out to his yurt, which I did on many occasions. I drove out there when there was paperwork to be signed. I drove out there to let him know every time I scheduled a showing. I drove out there when we received offers. And, yes, we received more than one offer. I always prayed on the way there that I would not find Barry taking a bath outside in his bathtub on cinderblocks.

I did, eventually sell that property for Barry and understand that he is now living on a beach in Hawaii in a tent.

· · · ● · · ● · · · ·

If some of those places were not bad enough, I did have my occasional interesting or entertaining client. On one occasion, I had a new client, Greg, who wanted to see remote, off-grid properties only. Greg was about six feet tall with a muscular build and wore silver-framed glasses. He had short dark hair and wore black fitted t-shirts and jeans. The first thing I noticed, was that he had a very peculiar way of looking at people that gave me the creeps. He was soft-spoken but would intensely stare at me like he was trying to see into my soul. He reminded me of a psycho-serial killer from a horror movie. I was definitely taking backup on these showings.

Lucas and Toby went with me the first day we looked at properties. There was one property Greg was super interested in, so we went there first. This property was near Clark Fork and had two or three off-grid alternatives. The house was built in the 1970s and was in excellent condition. It was mostly built of stone and a little wood. You could tell it was well-built. It was constructed over a creek that ran all year. You could hear that creek running from every room in the house.

The inside of the house also had a lot of stone work. There were two or three half-stone walls, separating different living areas, and a large stone fireplace with a woodstove insert. Both of the upstairs bedrooms had balconies overlooking the creek. Every room was immaculate and looked like they had never been touched.

The owner insisted on being there to show us how everything worked. His name was Mike and he had that clean-cut business executive appearance. He seemed to be in his late fifties and was very personable and professional. He had short wavy gray hair and wore jeans and a light blue Patagonia pullover sweater. From all outward appearances, he seemed like a regular guy. The more normal people that were around Greg with me, the better. He gave me the heebie jeebies.

First, there was a hydro-powered system, which supplied most of the power. Mike was an engineer and very proud of the system he designed and built. Mike spent forty-five minutes showing us how that worked. There were also solar panels and several large generators. Once we were inside the house, Greg, who was becoming increasingly odder and agitated, asked the owner, "So, what is your first line of defense should someone break into the house in the middle of the night?"

I was momentarily at a loss for words. *What is he doing? He is nuts.*

"Well," said Mike, "I would jump down behind that stone wall over there and hit that light switch while taking a shot like this."

Mike was now acting out this entire scene like we were on a movie set.

This went on for several minutes. *Oh my gosh, they are both nuts!* I shot my husband a look and he just rolled his eyes. Greg was surely someone you wanted to stay very aware of, but I was not sure he was a real threat. He was strange, all right. I had heard the term doomsday prepper but never really thought much about it or knew exactly what it meant. I had certainly never run across anyone like that in Virginia. These two guys were doing a good job of showing me what that entailed.

The owner, then took us to a hidden room in his basement, as if things could not get much weirder. This was his underground bunker, and it was constructed and stocked so that he could live in it and sustain himself for up to three months if needed. The door, which was no more than a wall that moved, sealed from the inside. He also had a locked safe in this bunker, which he opened to show us his display of every kind of firearm you could imagine and tons of ammunition. Greg was completely in awe of this. This guy was prepared for some sort of Armageddon. He and Greg were two peas in a pod, and I could not wait until we were done looking at properties that day.

We looked at several other places that day and decided to look at several more over the following week. I made sure to have Lucas and Toby with me every time. Eventually, Greg put an offer on a forty-acre piece of bare land. By then, my broker had met him several times and agreed that he probably was not a threat, just odd. Before closing on that property, Greg wanted to go out and walk it one more time. I agreed. Lucas was not available that day, so I made sure to carry my concealed gun and remember everything Sean had taught me.

As we were walking on the property, Greg asked me question after question about how remote this piece of property really was. I kept wondering, *What is this guy's deal? Is he running from someone?* I kept assuring him, it was about as remote as you can get in this part of Idaho.

I asked him if he had ever read the book or seen the movie *The Falcon and the Snowman.* He had not. I explained that it was a true story about a guy who had sold US security secrets to the Soviet Union years ago. The book came out in 1979, so it happened before that. I had heard that to avoid capture, he hid out for years in the mountains surrounding Bonners Ferry. In fact, I had also heard a story about him coming into town every week and having lunch with the sheriff, who had no idea who he was. I wasn't sure how much of that was actually true, but I was trying to give Greg a sense of how remote this area was.

He then said, "Why don't we go back to the office and talk to one of the men about it?"

Did he really just say that? I thought my head was going to explode. I felt he was questioning my ability because I am a woman. That is a major trigger point for me. To say I felt offended would be an understatement. I was good at what I did, and he was questioning me. I could feel my blood boiling as I struggled to try to remain professional. At that moment, I envisioned myself going all Uma Thurman, as in the movie *Kill Bill,* on him.

Instead, "If you would like," was all that came out of my mouth, while trying hard to bite my tongue.

We continued walking all over the rest of that property. The whole time, Greg was trying to identify every type of animal scat. For some reason, that was what he was obsessed with that day. *Does he think he is Bear Grylls, trying to impress me?* I just wanted to wrap this up and get back to the office. At one point, after seeing what he determined to be grizzly bear scat, he said, "I sure hope you are carrying." I assumed that was about the supposed wildlife on that remote piece of land but was not entirely sure.

Oh, I am, Greg. I am. I let him walk in front of me on the narrowing animal trail. I never replied to his comment, and I never let my guard down with him. The whole time I was thinking that I could probably shoot him if I was threatened, or had half a good reason. I was not so sure I could shoot an animal as easily. I was very glad when we finally closed on that property.

· · · · ●·●·● · · ·

I certainly saw some interesting places and met some interesting people in that job. I could not believe the way some people lived. Coming from where we lived in Virginia, it was an eye-opener. Several people I met lived in off-grid yurts or old campers turned into living quarters with woodstoves. I even showed one house that had a six-inch diameter hole in the plywood kitchen floor, which exposed the dirt crawl space underneath. It smelled so bad that the owner, who was living there, explained that, at one point, his mother had chickens and goats living freely in the house with her. I cannot imagine how bad that must have smelled because it already stunk terribly.

On one occasion, clients of mine, a very pleasant retired couple from Coeur d'Alene, who were looking for a large piece of property to build on, decided they wanted to see a questionable property on top of a mountain. I say "questionable" because I had heard many different rumors about that property but decided to keep those to myself until I saw it firsthand. Lucas and Toby accompanied me on the showing.

The road there was treacherous, to put it mildly. It was a private road that traversed the side of the mountain. There had been little to no maintenance done on it in over twenty years. Parts of it were eroding, and the entire road was slanting toward a drop-off down the mountain, which made us question if we should even continue to the top.

What we saw when we got there was a whole other world. There were some structures there, but we didn't think they were habitable. There was a very large underground bunker with numerous rooms, leading up to a huge room with about a thirty-foot ceiling. There were various pieces of hospital equipment lying around. There was broken rebar sticking out of crumbling cement walls and trash everywhere. In addition, there was an awful smell coming from somewhere inside this bunker. I felt like I was on the set of *Chernobyl*, waiting for some big mutant animal to emerge at any time from around the corner.

The story about this property was that there had been a group of people who were very worried about Y2K. They got together, bought, and built this place to sustain life. Rumor had it that there were delivery rooms here for pregnant women. When Y2K did not happen, that group of people eventually went bankrupt and abandoned it. Subsequently, a group of squatters moved in, staying for years and trashing the whole place before being forced out. Owners then built a fence to block access from the bottom of the mountain. This place was certainly unique.

My clients decided it would cost way too much money to do anything with this property. I agreed. While walking through an underground room on our way out, using our iPhone lights, a very large animal ran across the hallway in front of us. It was the size of a basset hound and looked like a rat. There it was, the mutant animal I had been fearing.

Toby went after it.

"Toby, get back here," I yelled.

"Toby, come," hollered Lucas.

Within a couple of seconds, he came running back and stood behind us, looking back in the direction he had just come from. Something had spooked my big brave boxer. That was it, we got the heck out of there, and those clients never called me to look at property again.

· · · · • · • · · ·

Not all the properties in this area are sketchy. There are some beautiful homes with awesome views. There are, however, good views from almost anywhere in north Idaho. Bonners Ferry is a little-known, gorgeous, outdoorsy place to live, where the cost of living is still reasonable, which makes it a desirable place to retire to.

In addition to the, shall I say, interesting people I crossed paths with, I also met many wonderful people who ended up buying property here, and in the process, have become good friends.

13

Spring in Idaho

Our first winter was not as cold and snowy as we had expected. Nothing ever shut down due to snow, and the roads were always well-plowed. That following spring, we managed to convince my parents to move out. They arrived in September, and of course, we had record amounts of snow their first winter, resulting in my mom falling on ice and breaking both of her wrists. They reminded me frequently that I told them winters were not so bad.

That following spring was also memorable. After having huge amounts of snow that winter and now a big melt with warmer temperatures coming, fields and creeks were flooding.

Our driveway and horse field were nothing but deep mud.

Mom and Dad were planning on coming for dinner one night. They lived just north of Bonners Ferry that first year, where we found them a nice little rancher with great views of the mountains. That afternoon, they needed to run to the grocery store. Mom was planning on making the dessert and needed a few things. On their way home, traffic was stopped from before the bridge in Bonners Ferry, all the way back to the Super One, about a half of a mile. This was very unusual. There were never any traffic issues, especially compared to traffic around Washington, DC. After sitting still for about forty-five minutes, Dad finally got out of his car and spoke to another driver.

Apparently, due to the large amounts of rapidly melting snow, there had been a mudslide right before the bridge, and mud had completely blocked the highway in both directions. No one seemed to have any idea how long it was going to take to clear it. There was no other way to get to the north side of town without driving a couple of hours south and then east into Montana and continuing up and around. Traffic stayed at a standstill for over three hours. At one point, the restaurants and coffee shops along the side of the road started bringing out water, coffee, and snacks for people, which I thought was a very nice gesture. I was starting to love this small-town community of Bonners Ferry.

Once the road finally opened again, it was getting dark. We decided to put dinner off until the next day.

Later that night, I was checking the local Facebook page for any news regarding the mudslide and came across a new one just south of town. It was so big that there was now a ten-foot-high wall of mud across Highway 95. No one was hurt, but it did push one car with a young mom and her two children completely off the road. Highway 95 is the only highway in Idaho that goes from Canada to Boise. They had no idea how long it was going to be closed. The possibility of mudslides in north Idaho had never occurred to me. I wondered if this was a common occurrence.

A couple of nights later, I was sitting by the window on our couch watching TV with Lucas. Lucas had fallen asleep, as usual. I noticed this bright flash of light, like lightning, out the window, and when I looked, it lasted longer than lightning and seemed to be more like a streak of light traveling pretty fast in a northern direction. It seemed more like it was falling out of the sky. *What the heck?* It lit up the entire sky for a moment. I could not imagine what that was. The next morning, I read that a meteor had hit the ground in Canada, just over the border from us.

North Idaho was full of surprises. Mom and Dad were a little unsure of what they had moved to but were committed to staying for the time being.

• • • • • • • • • • •

This was the same spring Copper became lame. He initially started tripping when we were on trails in the mountains. He then fell a few times with me on him but always managed to keep me from getting hurt. I started to become concerned. I also noticed that he seemed to be limping, especially when walking downhill. I scheduled an appointment with Dr. Derek.

After a thorough exam and X-rays, he determined that Copper had developed some arthritis in his pastern in his front right leg. The pastern is like an ankle. He had noticeable swelling in the front of that joint. Dr. Derek said I could ride him if I gave him Bute prior to riding. In my mind, I felt like that was the equivalent of giving my eighty-five-year-old father Advil and then telling him to go shovel the driveway. It was obvious how much Copper was hurting. Watching him limp made me want to cry at times. The downhills seemed to bother him a lot more than the uphills or flats, and now I understood why. I know he would've continued to carry me in those mountains if I asked him too. However, I did not have the heart to continue to do that. I loved him too much. I would retire him and just love on him and spoil him as much as I could. He was my first and will be my forever horse.

• • • • • • • • • • •

It was now time for me to find another horse. Lucas had trained Stella, our young mare who came with Copper. He was riding her. She was turning out to be an exceptional horse. Stella was also a Missouri Fox Trotter and had been with Copper since she was born. She was actually his niece, and she was only six years old. She was taller and fuller-bodied than any of our other horses. Lucas had done a great job training her.

Lucas found a horse online he thought might work for me, and it was not far from us. The owners were not going to be available to show him until the following weekend. Lucas was scheduled to be out of town over the weekend but suggested I go and look at him anyway. If I liked him, we would make arrangements to purchase him.

I took Katey with me. I just felt better having another person's opinion, plus she knew a lot more about horses than I did. This horse, Cody, was slightly smaller than Copper, a registered quarter-horse, and very well trained. I rode him in their round pen and then took him in the woods behind their property by myself. He did fine. I asked Katey if she would also ride him, just to make me feel better. She did and thought he was great.

I called Lucas later that afternoon and we decided to go ahead and purchase Cody.

Katey brought her trailer over the next morning and took me to pick him up. Once we got home, she suggested that instead of turning him out with the other three horses, I should separate them, allowing them to meet over the fence first. I thought that was a great idea. So, that is what I did. Copper, Stella, and Shaker had the full fenced ten acres, and Cody had the smaller, quarter acre with a run-in shed.

Since it was late spring and the weather was getting darn near perfect out, I had the windows open all night. The temps had been in the fifties all night and were forecasted to be in the mid-seventies that day. The sun was already up, and it was completely light outside by 5 a.m., as it is that time of year.

At 5:15, I awoke to what sounded like a stampede of buffalo right outside my bedroom window. I jumped up and looked outside. Somehow, Cody was in the big field and the other three horses were chasing him all over the field. Shaker was leading the charge. For being lame, Copper was doing a pretty good job of keeping up with them too. How in the heck did Cody get out? *Oh crap, and Lucas is still out of town.*

I jumped out of bed, into my muck boots, and ran down to the barn. Cody had been penned up right next to it. The metal cattle panel gate separating him from the other horses was lying on the ground and completely bent up. I had no idea how any of those horses did that. I did not know of any animal that was even capable of bending a metal gate like that, except maybe an elephant. I stood there looking at it, trying to figure out how this happened when Cody came running down over the hill, toward me. I heard the rest of them gaining on him. I yelled, "Come on Cody. Hurry up. That a boy!" as I dragged the bent gate out of the way.

When he saw me, he picked up his pace, as if he were saying, thank God you are here. I opened the gate going into the barn and shooed him right in there, closing that gate behind me. I put Cody in a stall and noticed several superficial bites and kick marks on him. Other than that, he seemed to be physically okay. Poor guy. I did not have the faintest idea of what to do next. It was 5:30 a.m. on a Sunday, and I needed help. I hated to bother Katey, but did not know who else to call.

"Katey, I am so sorry to bother you, but I need help. My other three horses broke down the gate, and it is all mangled. They have been chasing Cody for the last half an hour. I finally got him in the barn but am not sure if this gate is even salvageable."

"I am on my way," Katey said, as she hung up.

She was there within five minutes, in her pajamas and muck boots, assessing the damage to the gate. I had been thinking about how we could construct a makeshift gate until Lucas came home but could not come up with anything. Katey thought she could fix it. I had serious doubts. She then asked me for a tool I had never heard of. I cannot recall the exact name of it; suffice to say it was not your typical hammer, screwdriver, pliers, or wrench. I brought her into Lucas's shop and showed her all his tools. She grabbed several things and we headed back out.

I helped Katey pick up the gate and hold it in the correct position, as she pounded on her side of it with various tools. The gate was heavy and awkward for one person, as it was large. She then told me that whoever put that gate on originally installed it upside down. Well, Lucas did that. Lucas was extremely skilled at building things and could do just about anything. He was also a little anal about doing things correctly. I had to chuckle. Katey was now correcting the way Lucas constructed our fence and gate. After this, I would never question Katey's ability to do anything. I couldn't believe it, but she straightened that gate out and put it back in perfect working condition. I never could've done that. This short, little, unassuming woman could do anything. She certainly had saved me that morning.

She then looked at me and said, "Now, here is what you are going to do. You are not putting Cody back in here, just on the other side of the fence from the rest of them. You are going to put him across the driveway, in your round pen, until Lucas comes home."

"But, I don't have another water tank for him."

"I will lend you one. Let's go get it now."

Damn. She is good. Talk about a self-sufficient woman.

After I got back home and set the new water tank up for Cody, I had to laugh. At 5:30 on a Sunday morning, there were two middle-aged women, in their pajamas and muck boots, fixing a downed livestock fence with no man in sight. The fact that we, mostly Katey, were able to fix it, made me feel proud. Just a couple of years ago, I would have been sitting on my back porch, having a cup of coffee, waiting for my kids to get up so I could make them breakfast. Now they were off to college and there I was.

· · · • · • · · ·

Around that time, Lucas was developing a fascination with mules. This was another result of Lucas having too much idle time while I was working. He found two mules for sale in Montana that he was fairly interested in. He suggested we go and see them. I did not share his enthusiasm for mules but would ride along to appease him. Unfortunately, Cody had not worked out for a number of reasons, and I was still looking for a horse.

Saturday morning, on our drive to Montana, I asked Lucas why he was so interested in mules lately? I really could not understand it. I have always heard that mules were stubborn. Lucas is about the most stubborn man I know. How was that going to work?

"Because they live, on average, about ten years longer than a horse, you can ride them about ten years longer than a horse, and they are supposed to be way more sure-footed in the mountains and have more endurance."

"There is nothing wrong with Stella," I said.

"No. There is not. I am just curious about mules for the type of riding we do. In addition," Lucas added, "both mules have experience packing (which is hauling gear into the mountains), and I would like to help the local Forest Service with that in the summertime."

I began to realize that Lucas needed stimulation and adventure to occupy himself and stay happy. He was seldom ever content. *Maybe he needs medication of some sort.*

"And, the downside to a mule is?" I asked.

"I have been reading up on that. Apparently, you cannot make a mule do something it does not want to do like you can with a horse."

"Oh, and my husband is okay with that?" I said loudly, with a hint of sarcasm.

If we end up with a mule, I could imagine Lucas, who is the most stubborn person I have ever met, and a mule having stand-offs about doing certain things. Lucas is not always the most patient man either.

"Abby, I have also read that mules do not spook like a horse can."

Well, that could be good. Both Copper and Stella, as well as a few others we have briefly owned during this process, have spooked, or startled, when noticing something new on a trail. The worst thing they had ever done was startle and then spin around. None of our horses had ever taken off with us.

"Just keep an open mind, Abby."

As we pulled onto the property where the mules were, we noticed the two of them right away. One was black and one was white. They were running along the fence next to our car, braying. I had to admit, they were kind of cute. They were shorter than our horses, but much stockier. Their heads and, of course, their ears were much larger. We got out of the car and went over to the fence. They certainly were friendly fellas, and did not seem to mind their ears being touched like I had heard some mules did. As the owner and his wife came out of the house, the mules left us and went to greet them.

"I see you have already met Thor and Winston."

"Yes. They sure are friendly fellas," hollered Lucas.

We found out they really did not want to sell these guys, but they needed the money for medical bills. They had had them since they were babies, and they were part of their family. More than anything,

I think they just wanted to find them a good home. I couldn't help but feel sorry for them.

After spending a good hour checking them over and taking them on short rides down the driveway and back, Lucas decided we had to have them. By now, the owner was comfortable with us taking them and offered to throw in their saddles. Apparently, mule saddles are different from horse saddles. The deal was done. Lucas gave them a down payment and made arrangements to come and pick them up the next day.

Once we were back in the car, I asked Lucas, "What is the plan for these mules? Are you going to ride both of them and Stella?"

"No. I was thinking that the white one, Thor, would be good for you instead of a horse. Maybe I will ride both Stella and Winston."

"Really? Are you going to work with Thor before I get on him and take him on a few trail rides first because I am not the one who wanted a mule?"

"Yes, I will do that for you."

"Okay. I will try him," I agreed, still feeling a little skeptical.

Riding a mule had never been something I wanted to do, and somehow, my next horse was now a mule. I would try to keep an open mind. Maybe I would find I liked mules.

• • • ● • ● • • •

Lucas worked with those mules every day for the next two weeks, and they seemed to be progressing well. At other times, it seemed he had his work cut out for him. For instance, Winston did not like being loaded into the trailer. Since we trailer our horses and mules to the trail heads every time we ride in the mountains, this was something Lucas had to fix.

One sunny morning, while making a cup of coffee, I noticed Lucas trying to get Winston in our trailer. Lucas had gotten up early to work with him before it got too hot out. Winston was not having any of it. Every time Winston refused, Lucas made him run in circles for a few minutes and would then ask him again. Winston would refuse again. This went on long after I was done drinking two cups of coffee—at least an hour. If I had to bet on who would break first,

I really had no idea who to pick. I knew my husband well enough to know once he started something like this, he would not quit. I finally walked down to see if I could help.

"Abby, do me a favor and just stand behind him and tap him on the butt with the lunge whip when I ask him to load."

I got behind Winston. He turned his head, took one look at the lunge whip, and stepped right into the trailer. I never had to touch him with it. I would like to think that Winston did that for me. In reality, he was probably just tired of running in circles. Turns out mules are both stubborn and smart.

· · · · ● · ● · · · ·

On other occasions, both mules seemed to be doing great. They knew all their basic commands but would sometimes test Lucas to see what they could get away with, which was no different from most horses. Lucas was always right on top of it. Both Thor and Winston were super friendly and sweet. They both had a very strange habit of standing at the fence rail, taking four steps back, then four steps up to the fence, then four steps back. They would stand next to each other doing this for thirty minutes at a time and never more than four steps in either direction. We were never sure if it was a nervous thing, or they were just bored.

One day, I was in the pen with them, when they started doing this. I got between them and started doing it with them while I counted. One, two, three, four, one, two, three, four. It looked like we were doing a line dance. When Lucas drove by in his tractor, he just shook his head.

A little later that day, Lucas asked if I was ready to try riding Thor on a short trail ride behind our house. I said sure. As we were riding the mules up the driveway and behind the house, I liked the fact that Thor was a little shorter than other horses I had tried. It was less distance to fall to the ground. He seemed sweet but could be a little difficult to steer sometimes. I think he wanted to go his way, not mine. I just had to be tougher with him. This will be an interesting ride, for sure.

As we wound our way up the game trails on the mountain behind our house, things were going well for the first thirty minutes. We were following Lucas and Stella. As we got to a part where there was a pretty tight series of small switchbacks, I held Thor back to give Stella a little breathing room. I could see Thor watching her every move. Once she got to the top of the switchbacks, it was our turn. I nudged Thor forward and HE decided that we were not doing all that extra work. We were now going straight up the side of this steep incline. The hell with the switchbacks. *Damn mule!*

"Oh, my God. Oh, my God. Oh, my God," I kept saying as I was dodging tree branches and bushes with my head while laying down on his neck and hanging on for dear life.

Once we reached Lucas, and I knew I was safe, I could not help by laugh a little. He grinned and said, "Abby, you have to control him better than that."

"Yeah, okay." *As if I really have a choice.*

The rest of that ride was great until we came back down those same switchbacks. Again, Thor obviously did not think he needed to take the switchbacks. We came straight down that steep incline and brought a good-sized pine tree with us, between his legs. This was one crazy mule who had a mind of his own, and I was just a passenger.

"Abby, what are you doing? Make him use the switchbacks."

"I tried," I hollered. "It's not happening."

A couple of days later, we decided to try a different trail with Thor. Again, we were following Lucas on Stella. The trail we were on was narrow, sandwiched between an embankment and pine trees. We had been on the trail for about an hour and were now heading back home. This ride was going much better than the first one. Thor seemed to be a perfect gentleman and did everything I asked him to do. At least, until I heard a loud commotion in the pine trees right next to us and Thor decided it was every mule for himself. He pushed by Lucas and Stella, shoving them into the embankment, and took off running down the trail. This is the second time I have had a horse or mule take off with me, and it still was not a good feeling. I screamed for Lucas as we blew by him. I finally got Thor to stop about fifty yards away on the trail. He stopped, but he was marching in place, obviously agitated. I was doing my best to calm him down.

"What was that?" I hollered to Lucas.

"It was a bear that we scared up a tree," Lucas said as he tried to keep Stella under that tree so he could get a better look at the bear. She was also dancing nervously.

Holy Cow! We were just a couple of feet away from a bear! Thor was now really prancing in place, and I was using all my strength to hold him back from taking off again. In addition, Lucas seemed more concerned with seeing the bear than saving me on a runaway mule.

"Lucas, let's get out of here. We don't need to meet the bear in person," I yelled.

As Lucas caught up with us, I said, "I thought mules were not supposed to spook at things?"

"Yeah. Well, I guess that was different. To him, maybe it was self-preservation."

I would try riding Thor a few more times. Each time resulted in him deciding that he was in charge at some point, either by taking a different route, jumping a creek instead of walking through it, or going straight down a mountain instead of using the trail, and Lucas was getting more frustrated with me for not controlling Thor better. I started to feel like I was not a strong enough rider for Thor or Lucas, but was not ready to give up.

· · · · • · • · · ·

That summer, we joined the Back Country Horsemen of north Idaho, hoping to find some people we could ride with. On our first ride with new friends from this group, I took Thor. I was determined to make things work with him. Lucas was particularly excited to get to know some of these people. I suspected he was looking for some more experienced people to ride with, other than just me. However, this ride was doomed from the minute I got Thor off the trailer and he dragged me across the parking lot to some nice tall grass he was interested in.

"Abby, yank on his lead line and get him back here," Lucas snapped.

"I have been and he doesn't seem to care what I do. He is much stronger."

After tying his horse up, Lucas had to grab Thor and seemed mildly frustrated with me already. Maybe he was embarrassed. I am not sure.

We saddled everyone up and started on the trail with our group of eight people. On a newer horse or mule, I am most comfortable riding in the back of the group. It gives me a little piece of mind that they will not run off with me. On this day, Thor seemed antsy and wanted to walk a little faster, so we were out in front, getting further and further in front of the rest of the group. Every time I tried to stop him to wait for the group, he would prance and turn in place. I was starting to feel like I was losing control of him again, and that was starting to scare me.

Eventually, we ended up back in the middle of the group on some large switchbacks, climbing the side of the mountain. When Lucas and Stella were on the switchback directly above us, Thor decided to take a shortcut and go right up the mountain to catch up with them. There was nothing I could do to stop him. I just hung on. Thor cut right in front of the rider behind Lucas, as I apologized. Lucas kept giving me looks but didn't say anything. I could tell how annoyed he was with me.

We finally made it to the top of the mountain, stopped, tied up the horses, and had lunch with the group. I was very glad for this break. We enjoyed lunch with the group while admiring the amazing view from the top of this mountain. Everyone seemed very nice and had way more riding experience than I did. Not one of them rode a mule. I had the only mule on this ride.

As we were getting ready to mount up and start back down the mountain, Lucas decided to take Stella away from the rest of the group and cut through some trees on a steep incline. He said he would meet the rest of us, me included, on the trail below. I was not sure if he was trying to work on getting Stella okay with leaving the group, or if he was so annoyed and embarrassed by me, that he needed space.

Horses are herd animals and always want to stay with the pack or their buddies. Thor was now beside himself because Stella, his buddy, had left our group. He kept trying to follow Lucas down the embankment, and I kept trying to stop him from doing it. I knew I had to get control of him, and fast. I was really trying. At one point, he backed me into a large pine tree, probably trying to knock me off of him. My anxiety levels were rising rapidly, and I was no longer enjoying this day. I was positive Thor was feeling my anxiety. Lucas was now a good distance down the hill and away from us. *Damn him. He left me up here with this crazy-ass mule. I didn't want a mule in the first place!*

Luckily, one of the other riders noticed my predicament, and she came over to help. She grabbed Thor's lead line, yanked on it to get his attention, and started to pony us around the embankment. While I was so grateful for this help and didn't care if I looked like a silly novice rider at that moment, Thor was beside himself although he really did not have a choice.

Once we got down to the trail and I briefly had control of Thor again, he kept trying to pass all the other horses, so he could catch up with Stella and Lucas. The trail was way too narrow to pass on, and there was a steep drop-off on our right. I kept fighting with him. Several times, he turned and backed up. I believed we were going to go backward off the cliff, so I jumped off him while he was moving. That would always result in everyone stopping until I could get him straightened out and get back on.

I was struggling, and Lucas was beyond frustrated with me. The last time I jumped off him, just before his back feet slipped off the cliff, I slipped and slid underneath him. My feet were now hanging over the cliff. Realizing I was in a very precarious position, somebody behind me grabbed my mule and held him still until I could get out from under him, which I quickly did. Thor then managed to right himself on the trail again. That was it! I was done!

I was scared to death to finish riding Thor off this mountain. I was also royally pissed at Lucas. I didn't care what Lucas or anybody else thought. I was contemplating being done with riding all together. Fighting back tears, I decided to walk the seven miles we had left, when one of the other guys on the ride, Paul, offered to ride my mule and offered me his horse to ride out. I said no at first but then agreed.

Paul was an exceptionally good rider. Once he was on Thor, I saw him struggling just like I had been. After a few minutes, I heard him say to Lucas, "Lucas, this mule is pretty hard to handle."

Thank you, Paul, for coming to my defense. That was the last time I rode Thor. I felt like a failure. I was not a strong enough rider to control a mule, and we could not seem to find another horse for me.

· · • · ♦ · • · · ·

At this point, I was ready to quit riding altogether. I was never going to be a strong enough rider in Lucas's eyes to do the things he wanted to do. Lucas, not knowing what else to do, suggested I take Stella, and he would ride Thor and Winston. Winston was not an option for me. According to Lucas, he was a little harder to handle than Thor.

In addition to Thor, we had tried out a couple of other horses, who had various issues. Cody would not tie, meaning he would pull back, breaking his lead line, and flip over backward almost every time we tried to tie him up. One time resulted in stitches in his head. Another horse would not cross a bridge or water for anything. We cross lots of water and many bridges in these mountains. If we pushed this guy to cross water too much, he would leap seven feet in the air over it. Obviously, that was not going to work. A third one, Buddy, seemed to be okay half of the time. The other half the time, he seemed to decide, for no particular reason, that he didn't want to continue whatever ride we were on, and he would stop, refusing to take another step. Lucas, thinking I was just not being assertive enough, finally got on him and tried to make him go, which resulted in Buddy throwing his head back and cracking Lucas in the face, giving him a bloody nose. We had Buddy checked out by vets, to see if something was hurting him. We even took him to an equine chiropractor for several treatments. Nothing seemed to make a difference, and we couldn't find anything wrong with him. We figured he just had a screw loose and ended up selling him.

I had never been on Stella. Lucas had spent the last few years training and working with her. My first thought was, *She is really tall, and that is a long way to the ground if I fall.* She was big, sixteen hands, strong and athletic. She was similar in build to that barrel racing horse who took off with me a few years earlier. I was a little apprehensive. I did not want to admit it, but I felt like I was starting to regress and lose my confidence in riding altogether. Lucas finally convinced me to try her.

After a handful of rides on her, Lucas was never getting Stella back. She was my horse now, and she was so good at keeping me safe. Lucas had done a fantastic job of training her. With the right horse, my confidence in riding increased exponentially. I never hesitated to ride Stella anywhere, and I thanked God for her every day. I started to develop a strong trust in her, similar to Copper.

Stella would eventually show me exactly what I was capable of.

14

Stella

After acquiring Stella from Lucas, on more than one occasion, I found myself in situations in the mountains where I was not sure how we were going to proceed. Stella was able to do just about anything and consistently amazed me. For example, one time we were riding on a trail in early spring. Many times, the trails are not cleared by the Forest Service until early summer. We came upon a large tree that had fallen across the trail. This one was too big for our horses to step or jump over. We had to find another way. We decided to try to go around it, which entailed walking through some thick brush and stepping over other downed trees. None of that was a problem for Stella. Once we got close to the trail, in front of that downed tree, there was a thick line of pine trees blocking our path to the trail. They were about six feet tall on average and too close together to walk between. I could not see a way to the trail from there. As we were standing there contemplating our next move, I mumbled, "Now how are we going to get over there?"

The next thing I knew, Stella was plowing the pine trees to the ground and walking right over them. She stopped on the trail as if to say, "That is how we are going to do it. I got this."

She made me laugh. I swear, I think she understood most of what I said.

· · · • · • · • · ·

Another time, we were following a narrow switchback up the side of a mountain. There were four of us relatively close together. On one of the turns, which was tight, there was another large tree across the path. There was no way we were going to get around this one. In addition, the horses did not have enough room to turn around, and backing up on this narrow curve could be sketchy. Stella and I were third in line. As I looked at the steep, brushy incline from where we were to the trail above us, which was in front of that downed tree, Stella turned and hesitated, as if she was asking, "Do you want me to do this? I am sure I can."

"Ok, Stella," I said, as I spurred her on, and up we went.

"Abby, good Lord!" cried Lucas.

I just smiled, having given everyone else room to turn around on that trail and start back down the mountain. Stella and I went back down the embankment and took up the end of the line. Stella never had any problems, and she and I began to really trust each other. Like Copper, I knew she would take care of me.

· · · • · • · • · ·

There was a time when we were coming back down from a seventeen-mile mountain ride. I was with Lucas and another friend of ours, Sherry. For some reason that day, there were several pretty rough water crossings, and none of the horses wanted to cross them. The only one who would do it willingly was Stella. Not realizing this ride was as long as it was until we were at the top, we tried to take a shortcut back down. We came up on about a fifteen-foot-wide creek crossing. To get to the creek, we had to go down a very steep and narrow path, which was mostly large boulders.

Lucas was now riding a young horse, who was struggling across streams. Sherry was riding our other horse who sometimes panicked in water. Lucas told me to go first, thinking that if Stella crossed, the others would follow her. He stayed close behind me. We got halfway down that embankment and Stella refused to go any further. I could immediately see why. There was a good-sized tree growing out of the side of the embankment, and while Stella might fit under it, there was no way I was going to get under that from on top of Stella. Lucas was now right up against Stella's butt.

"Abby, you have to go. Move. You can't stand here," Lucas snapped with a real sense of urgency in his voice.

"Lucas, we can't go forward because of this tree."

Due to the steepness, there was nowhere for either of us to go. We couldn't back up and we couldn't go forward.

"Well then, get off and walk her across the creek."

"Where exactly do you want me to get off? To my right is about a ten-foot drop down to a big boulder and there is an extremely steep, vertical wall of dirt on my left." The trail was so narrow that there was not enough room to stand next to a horse.

"I don't care. You can't stay like this," he said, getting increasingly annoyed with the situation.

In fairness, Lucas would have had a hard time backing up that steep, narrow part of the trail. Yet, I knew that if the situation was reversed and I was behind Lucas like that, he would be so upset with me for being right up on his butt. However, it was not the time to start squabbling. Lucas was getting very agitated, so I attempted to get off on my left and stand on the dirt wall. As soon as my second foot hit the dirt, I completely lost my footing and slid directly underneath Stella.

"Please, Stella, do not move," I pleaded until I figured out my next move.

That was the second time I found myself on the ground lying underneath my horse or mule. I climbed down to the boulder below us and attempted to lead Stella down the path of large wet boulders to cross this creek. I held my breath with every step she took, knowing it was super slippery, and I did not want anything to happen to her. We made it across and so did Lucas and Sherry. Thank God.

There was one bigger river to cross before getting back to our trailer that day. Again, it was nothing but large wet boulders all the way across. Not ideal. At one point, I had heard there was a bridge there, but it had since washed away. That had to be the scariest-looking water crossing for horses I had ever seen. The water was running fast between large boulders, and it was hard to tell how deep it was in spots. *If we all make it across without an injury, it will be a miracle.* We did not have any other choices, other than to go back the way we came, and that would add another seven miles onto this fifteen-mile day. The horses were already exhausted.

Lucas decided to walk and lead his young horse across. They made it but not without slipping a few times. Once on the other side, there was an extremely steep incline to get back up the road. They made it up that also.

Sherry went next. She decided to ride our other horse, Scout, across. She tried a different route across the river, which resulted in her horse slipping several times, panicking, and falling over once with her on him in close to three feet of water. I have no idea how she stayed in the saddle while the horse righted himself up again, but she did. Her riding abilities always amazed me. They also made it up the steep incline.

I decided to ride Stella but go the same way Lucas had walked. I thought I would be safer on her, than on foot. Stella took her time, carefully looking where she was going to put each front foot. I was fine with that. She could take as long as she needed. We made it with no incidents.

Once we were on the other side, I noticed Sherry was standing behind Scout, whose entire back leg was skinned up and a bloody mess.

"Oh no! Is he okay?" I yelled.

She hollered, "He is okay. It's all superficial." Although, it was obviously bothering him. He was holding his leg up in the air, poor guy. In addition, Sherry was now soaking wet.

Lucas's horse had lost a shoe in that crossing, so he could not ride him any further. We had two miles to go to get to the trailer. Scout was now limping. Luckily those two miles were on a dirt road.

"Abby, give me Stella. You and Sherry stay here with these two. I will ride Stella quickly back to the trailer and bring it here."

"Good idea."

Lucas sped off with Stella, while Sherry and I untacked our horses. Again, Stella had risen to the occasion.

Once we got everyone home, we cleaned and dressed Scout's back leg with padding and vet wrap. It took him two full weeks to recover from that. We gave the other two a full week off also.

• • • • ● • ● • • • •

On yet another occasion, Lucas and I had taken our horse and mule to Snow Lake. Snow Lake is a pretty good ride in the mountains around here. It has approximately ten water crossings on the way up and then again on the way back. It has wooden bridges to cross at the top in addition to some real rocky sections, where the horses need to do a sort of rock scramble while carrying us. This was becoming one of my favorite rides in north Idaho.

At 9:30 on a sunny July morning, we arrived at the trailhead with our trailer. Temps were in the seventies already. It was shaping up to be a beautiful day for a trail ride. We saddled up Stella and Thor. Lucas had decided to bring Thor on this ride. He was having much better luck with him than I had. Toby had come with us like he had started doing on most of these rides. Lucas asked if he thought we should bring our rain gear. I did not think we needed it. There was not a cloud in the sky. He, however, thought it would not hurt to tie it on the back of the saddles, so we did. We were wearing T-shirts and were plenty warm. We tied our saddlebags onto the saddles, and I put our packed lunches and water bottles in our bags. I was so glad to have finally gotten comfortable with a good horse. It made these days so much more enjoyable. The day was starting out to be perfect.

We started down the trail—Lucas in front riding Thor and Stella and I behind. The first couple of creek crossings were uneventful. With all the snow still melting on top of the mountains, the creeks were running a little bit higher and faster. That did not seem to bother Stella and Thor. Each time I got close to the water at these crossings, I could feel the colder air coming off them. It was refreshing. Everything was now blooming, and it felt like heaven. Toby was running ahead, chasing any grouse or other wildlife away, and then he would circle back to check on us. He never went too far from us. These were the days that made us so grateful we lived here.

The ride to Snow Lake, at the top of this mountain, was about as perfect as it gets. Once at the top, we tied up the horses, unpacked our lunches, and found a large fallen tree to sit on. While we ate, we enjoyed a view of the entire lake. The lake was a vivid blue-green color, and snowcapped mountain peaks surrounded it on three sides. The water was so clear we could see every fish and turtle for at least fifteen feet. The crisp air smelled of pine. We were the only ones up there. In fact, we had not seen another person all day. It's fairly common in these mountains to never see another soul all day. Stella and Thor enjoyed their rest and the apples I had packed for them. While we were eating, Lucas noticed the wind picking up a little and some dark storm clouds showing up over one of the mountain peaks. It hardly ever rains in the summer there. When it does, it usually lasts for about ten minutes, and we rarely got thunderstorms. We seemed to have had them weekly in Virginia in the summer, and I must admit, I do miss those at times. There is nothing like the smell of fresh rain after a good old thunderstorm.

With the storm looking imminent, we decided to start back down the mountain just in case the weather turned. We rode back over the wooden bridges and down over the rock scramble just as we felt the first raindrops. Lucas stopped in front of me and hopped off Thor.

"I am putting my rain gear on," he said.

I looked at the sky and was feeling very optimistic. "Ah, it's going to blow over in no time," I replied. I opted not to put my rain gear on.

We continued down the mountain as the rain picked up. Then the wind started, and the temps dropped to the fifties within a couple of minutes. I still thought it was going to blow over in a few minutes, although I was feeling a little chilled. We kept moving. As the rain picked up, I finally contemplated stopping and putting my rain gear on just as the golf ball-sized hail started falling. *Oh no!* Toby was running for any tree he could hide under, and Lucas wanted to start trotting down the mountain, hoping to get out quickly. There was no time to stop now.

Crack!!! There was a loud clap of thunder directly over our heads. I always wondered what would happen if we were riding our horses when a thunderstorm started. How would they react? I was about to find out. Not ten seconds later, there was a bright flash of lightning. This thunderstorm was directly over our heads, and it seemed the hail was getting bigger. Thor is now pulling Lucas toward any large tree he can find to get away from the hail. Stella is just trotting straight ahead. She seemed to have the same mindset as Lucas.

About fifteen minutes later, we were still directly under this storm and it was still raining and hailing. I was soaked to the bone and freezing. For a day that started as the perfect summer day, it now felt like late fall. Poor Toby was staying with us while trying to hide from the hail under any tree along the way. Thor was not happy. He was throwing his head around, wanting to take charge, and Lucas was not having that. Stella never broke her stride and was absolutely perfect.

When we finally got back to our truck and trailer, I felt like my hands were frozen onto the reins. Like I frequently do, I silently thanked God again for Stella. She was a gem!

· · • ● • ● • • · ·

The only thing I was hesitant to do with Stella, and still had not done, was lope on her. Lucas had told me when he was training her that she had a very big lope and getting into it felt like riding a jackhammer. A lope is like a run. Some horses have slow ones, and some have fast ones. However, a lope is not a gallop, or an all-out sprint. Apparently, Stella has a fast lope. Just before she gets into her lope, she does a weird trot that is super bouncy, like a jackhammer. Lucas could not figure out why she did this. He even had a friend, a roper in local rodeos who also did some horse training, ride her, and he said the same thing. No one could figure it out. It didn't really matter to me, since ninety-nine percent of the time, we were walking or trotting. On several occasions, Lucas had tried to get me to lope her. I would initially agree, just to chicken out at the last minute and put Stella into her fast gait instead. If he was frustrated with me, he didn't show it too much. I think Lucas had resigned himself to the fact that I would only do what I was comfortable with.

Lucas still had a growing fascination with mules and tried several different mules that summer. Mules are a different breed. They say that a mule will only bond with one person in his lifetime. I believe that now. Lucas was still looking for that one.

There would, however, be only one more mule in our lives, and a series of events caused by this guy would indirectly push me past everything I believed I was capable of.

15

Diego

After a few more rides with Thor, Lucas decided he was too much of a "lug head," as he put it. He was tired of constantly fighting with him for control on the trails. He wanted a mule that was a little easier to handle. We sold Thor to a lady in Oregon, who takes him riding almost every day and absolutely loves him. Lucas was now doing tons of research to find the perfect mule. He finally found what seemed to be the answer to his prayers.

Diego came to us from Ohio, where he had been working with a well-known mule trainer for a couple of years. That trainer agreed to have Diego shipped to us, using a hauler he personally knew. It was supposed to take five days for him to get from Ohio to Idaho. It ended up taking closer to fourteen days. Apparently, the hauler's truck broke down in Utah, which caused the delay. By the time Diego arrived, he was visibly underweight and more than a little apprehensive about his new surroundings. The poor guy had just been through an extremely stressful ordeal, and I wondered if he had been fed at all or just didn't eat because of the stress.

We put Diego in a temporary pen by himself for the first week. We wanted to let him settle in before introducing him to the other horses. At first, he wouldn't eat much and seemed a little skittish. I couldn't blame him after his recent trek across the country. Diego was all black with four white socks—very flashy. He was tall, thin, and unsure of everything around him. Lucas spent time with him every day, sometimes grooming him and other times just sitting in his pen with a cup of coffee and some horse treats, trying to establish a bond. Diego was slowly warming up to Lucas and even started to appear happy to see him each day. After about a week of this, Lucas felt it was time to introduce Diego to the rest of the herd.

On a warm sunny morning, after bringing the horses in for breakfast, we decided to walk Diego into the barn so he could meet the other horses, who were in their stalls. Lucas paused at each horse, letting them all meet Diego through the stall doors. With only one whinny from Stella, it appeared things were going to be fine. Stella whinnied at every new horse or mule we brought on the property. It seemed to be a mare thing. Things never escalated beyond that. We let Diego out in the field by himself for about an hour to learn the boundaries before letting the other horses join him. At first, he didn't want to leave us at the gate. Eventually, he started to explore his new surroundings. After half an hour, he discovered the large round bale of hay and started trotting around and kicking up his back feet. I was so glad to finally see him happy.

Since Copper was the oldest and the alpha horse, we let him out next. If he accepted Diego, it was a good bet the rest of the herd would also. After a brief pinning of the ears and Copper chasing Diego away from his spot around the hay, everything seemed fine. As always, Copper needed to show the new guy how things were. Next, we let Stella out. She went trotting over to Diego and whinnied again, as they were nose to nose, checking each other out. Then she turned and playfully kicked out her two back feet toward him as if letting him know that he was beneath her in the pecking order. I had heard that mules were always at the bottom of the pecking order. It certainly was true with this herd. After Copper and Stella accepted Diego, the rest of the horses were happy to accept him too.

Over the next several months, Lucas worked with Diego almost every day. He did tons of groundwork with him, even teaching him to lie down so Lucas could get on him that way. We started taking him out on short trail rides with us and quickly noticed that if Diego was second, third, or last in line, he had no issues out on the trails. However, if he was first, he seemed to spook at everything. The trails in north Idaho are steep, narrow, and covered with alder and brush—not exactly a place where spooky is an asset. In addition, plenty of grouse, turkeys, deer, elk, and a few other animals could pop out onto the trail from between trees or bushes at any moment. That happened on a couple of occasions with Diego.

Once a grouse flew out of the bushes when Diego was almost on top of him. That completely freaked the poor guy out, and after jumping and startling, he stood there shaking for several minutes. I was sure he had never seen grouse in Ohio, nor had he been on many trail rides before coming to us.

Another time, he stopped on the trail and refused to go another step. After a minute, we realized he was looking at an elk about two hundred yards away across the ravine. At least he didn't turn and run. I am sure he had never seen an elk before either. It was going to take some time on these trails before Diego got used to our wildlife.

On the first couple of rides, it was also apparent that Diego did not like to be separated from the other horses. If he fell too far behind, he wanted to run to catch up, and Lucas, not wanting Diego to be in charge, would struggle to hold him back. Mules are strong, and if a mule wants to go, it is nearly impossible to hold him back. Nonetheless, Lucas had high hopes for Diego and kept working with him. He was still young, only six years old, and he was getting used to so many new things.

Lucas decided that one way to work on these things would be to occasionally take Diego out on the trails by himself. I did not think that was such a good idea and told Lucas so. I felt it was not safe, at least not until Diego got a little more acclimated to the trails and our wildlife. That was going to take more time. I also knew that was an argument I was not going to win, so I let it be. Lucas was well aware of how I felt.

Lucas rode Diego on the trails on our property, the state land property just down the road, and sometimes on timber land just adjacent to our property. He even trailered him to a private wildlife preserve. He wanted him to be comfortable going anywhere. They would have several good rides in a row and then one where, for no apparent reason, Diego acted like the boogie man was around every tree. Instead of walking straight ahead on the trail, Diego would stop, prance, or want to turn around and hurry home. This frustrated Lucas. However, Lucas kept at it. Once again, it was the battle of the hard heads—Lucas vs. Diego. He was determined to make this mule a success.

All of this came to a climax one day when Lucas decided to take Diego on the timberland trails next to our property—by himself. This property had been partially logged several years ago, opening up all kinds of new trails yet leaving many downed trees, limbs, and debris everywhere. There were only a few places to access this land, and most of those accesses were from our property. This was great for us. It was like having an additional six-hundred-plus acres to ride on from our property, and we seldom saw another person. It was remote and perfect.

That morning, I went on a walk with Katey. We started walking together because we had both independently seen a mountain lion recently. In addition to walking with someone else, Lucas insisted I carry my 38-revolver just in case. I had it attached to the inside waistband of my jeans, which was a little uncomfortable but worth the peace of mind it gave me.

We were about two and a half miles from home, when my mom called me, sounding panicked.

"Abby, Lucas took Diego out by himself about forty-five minutes ago, and Diego just came running home without him."

"Wait. What?"

"Lucas took Diego out on the timberland about forty-five minutes ago, and Diego just came running home without him!" She repeated frantically.

"Mom, can you come and pick us up right now? We are down the street and around the corner."

"Yes, I am on my way."

I hung up and tried to think of a good reason for this. Maybe Lucas had tied Diego up somewhere and he broke free and ran home. That couldn't be right. Lucas would never have stopped to take a break while riding out by himself. I could not think of any other scenarios that made sense. I was trying very hard to suppress my rising anxiety.

I do not remember the ride back to our barn. I know I had several moments of sheer panic. I kept telling myself that there had to be a simple explanation and everything was going to be okay. Lucas had only had Diego for a couple of months, and they were still getting to know each other. The only questionable thing Diego had ever done was spook at elk or grouse. Even then, all Diego did was jump and startle. He never took off. I could not imagine why Diego left Lucas. I reminded myself that Lucas was an excellent rider.

Once we got back to the barn, Stella and Scout, our other horses, were saddled up and tied to the hitching post right in front of the barn. Lucas had started doing this for about an hour every day to teach them to stand quietly when tied. I was not a fan of that idea since they stood in the sun, during the heat of the day, with a saddle and full tack on, but I understood Lucas's logic. My dad had ahold of Diego, who was a sweaty anxious mess but seemed unharmed. Upon closer inspection, I noticed that one of Diego's reins was missing and Lucas's sunglasses were, somehow, broken and stuck between the horn and saddle. That was odd. In addition, there was a piece of Lucas's sweatshirt sleeve wrapped around the horn.

For the first time since Lucas started saddling and tying those horses every day, I was glad he had done it. I ran over to Stella, untied her, told my mom to take Toby inside her house, put a bridle on Stella, and jumped up. Katey was helping my dad with Diego. I knew I had to find Lucas.

Mom hollered, "Where are you going?"

"To find Lucas. Mom, which way did Diego come back from?" There were a dozen different ways we could access that property.

"I am not sure, but I think it was that direction."

That narrowed it down to about four different possibilities. We trotted over the hill. There are so many old logging trails and a lot of steep hilly terrain there. In addition, Lucas had cleared many smaller trails for us to ride on. We could ride for hours and never use the same trail twice. I had no idea where to start. I just knew I had to get going. *Damn it, Lucas!*

Stella and I started going up and down every trail on that side of the property. We trotted the whole time, only stopping occasionally to holler for Lucas. I was getting more and more worried that I would not find him, and if I did, what kind of shape was going to be in? After going up and down three of the trails, we were starting up the fourth and steepest one. Stella was getting a workout like none other. She loved Lucas almost as much as I did, and I knew she would never quit until we found him. We stopped at the bottom of the hill, and I hollered again. Nothing. Once we got halfway up the hill, we stopped and I hollered again. This time, I heard Lucas in the distance.

"Up here! I'm up here."

I also heard the unmistakable sound of a mountain lion's roar in the distance. It was coming from the top of the trail somewhere. Stella heard it at the same time. Her ears pointed toward the sound and then they flattened to her head as she gave a little muffled whinny. We needed to go quickly, and I instinctively knew what she was going to do. This was one of those times that I knew I had to trust Stella. At this point, we were operating as one entity, doing what we had to do for Lucas. We took off at a full sprint up the rest of that hill. I have never gone that fast on a horse, ever. My only thought was of getting to Lucas, I did not care how fast we had to go. I hung on.

Once we arrived, Stella stopped abruptly, jolting me in the saddle slightly. That is when I noticed the mountain lion. He was huge—as tall as a great dane, and heavier. He was about five feet away from Lucas who was half sitting and half lying on the ground with a big stick in his hand, trying to protect himself. I locked eyes with the lion, and he opened his mouth and growled at us but did not back away. *Holy Shit, they have big teeth!*

"Stellaaaa," I said, not knowing what else to do, and feeling scared out of my mind. At that, Stella lunged toward that mountain lion, with me on her, stomping her front feet at him the entire time. She was trying to protect us. He only backed away a few feet and then moved closer again. She did it again. The cat took this as a challenge and moved around to the other side of Lucas, inching closer.

"What the hell?" I yelled. I started waving my arms and hollering. "Get out of here! Go! Shoo!"

He would not budge. Stella and I were both at a loss for what to do.

The next moment, I remembered I had my gun. I put my hand on it and briefly considered the fact that Stella had never been close to gunfire, and if I were to shoot off the top of her, I could end up on the ground with Lucas with Stella running to the next county. It didn't matter. It was my only choice.

"Stella, easy girl," I said as I steadied her. I aimed my gun as best as I could with one hand and tightened my grip on the reins and horn with my other hand, bracing for whatever came next. All I was thinking about was getting that mountain lion out of there. I had no time to put my reader glasses on to aim that gun. I just aimed for the general vicinity of the cat and said a quick silent prayer. I pulled that trigger.

Stella startled and reared up slightly a few times before realizing she was okay. I managed to stay on her. I believe I missed hitting that cat by a mile. However, he took off running until he was completely out of sight. I was pretty sure he wasn't coming back anytime soon. I was certainly praying that was the case.

As my adrenaline continued to surge, I hopped off Stella and knelt next to Lucas, who was staring at me with his mouth open and eyes huge like he was in total shock. I figured it was because he had been terrified of that mountain lion. It never occurred to me that there was any other reason.

"Are you okay?" I asked.

"Yes. No," he said as if being jolted back to reality. "I mean my leg is broken. Other than that, I think so."

Getting my first real good look at Lucas and his injuries raised a whole new set of questions. Yes, his ankle was broken. I could tell that from the position his foot was in. He had several bruises already showing and minor cuts and scrapes on his face and arm. He had one black eye starting to show, and both wrists were swollen and sore. He did not think they were broken, but I wasn't so sure.

"How, in the world, are we going to get you out of here now?"

"I have no idea, Abby. If I can get on Stella, maybe I could ride out."

"Okay. How are we going to get you on Stella with that leg and your wrists?"

"I don't know," Lucas said, wincing while trying to move his leg.

We sat there for a minute, contemplating how we were to do this. I had no idea how to move him without jarring that ankle and having him, justifiably, scream with pain. We had to do something to splint it and keep it still. We had no cell service there, and I was not going to leave him to get help—not with that mountain lion in the area. With his swollen wrists, he would not even be able to shoot my gun.

"What the hell happened?" I asked.

Lucas explained that he and Diego had reached the top of this steep hill when the mule spooked at something. We knew by then that it was the mountain lion. Diego spun around, knocking Lucas off balance a little, and took off at an all-out gallop down the hill. Lucas said he had no idea a mule could run that fast. He hung to the side as long as he could. They had not gone very far when Diego jumped a culvert, and Lucas just let go. He knew he would not be able to hang on. His foot got temporarily caught in the stirrup and he was dragged a few feet. When he finally broke free, he landed in a pile of tree limbs and sticks. He was damn lucky he was not impaled.

By now, Lucas was starting to look very pale, like he was going into shock. I started to wonder if he had any internal injuries. I had to do something. Luckily, Stella still had her saddle bag attached to her saddle from the last time we rode in the mountains. I had a roll of vet wrap in there. I always kept a roll of it on longer rides in case of an emergency. It was not going to do much for Lucas's injuries, but maybe we could stabilize that ankle.

"Lucas, we have to somehow wrap up and stabilize that ankle enough to get you on Stella so you can ride out of here."

"Abby, I don't know how we are going to do that from the looks of my foot."

"I am not sure we have a choice, Lucas. Let me look at it. I promise I'll be careful."

I gently lifted his pant leg, afraid of what I might see. I was afraid to pull his sock down, worried that there might be too much pressure and cause more pain. I just felt his leg through his sock, very carefully. There didn't seem to be any bones sticking out. I didn't think it was a compound fracture, but there was no question it was broken. I have never seen a foot at that angle before. It was eerie. Between that and my sudden bolt of adrenaline, I was feeling a little queasy myself.

I looked around for some medium-sized branches. There weren't many that were not attached to much larger branches. I broke a few into what I thought would be the correct sizes. I took off my sweatshirt and very carefully wrapped that around his leg first. This was excruciating for Lucas, but I had no idea what else to do. I tried to move quickly and gently. I then placed the branches on either side of his leg, without moving the foot at all. Next, I had to wrap the vet wrap around all of this. Every time I lifted his leg slightly to get vet wrap under his leg, he winced and cursed. I wrapped it as tight as I could, hoping it would hold relatively still until we could get out of there.

Next, we had to figure out how to get him up on Stella. This was not easy. I pulled Stella close to us and tried to help Lucas stand up. Getting him standing was a slow and painful process, but he got there. Getting him on Stella was a different story. He could not put a foot in a stirrup, and I could not physically lift him up on her. Lucas is six feet one and weighs about 195 pounds. I have trouble lifting Stella's fifty-pound saddle onto her back. He is now standing with one hand on Stella's neck, using her to steady himself.

"Lucas, what if you grab onto the back of the saddle with your other hand, put your knee in my hands, and I will give you a boost? If we can do that, do you think you could swing your bad leg over the back of Stella?"

"I doubt it, Abby." Lucas was looking at me like I was crazy.

"Okay. What if we do the same thing from the other side of Stella and then you could swing your good leg over Stella?"

"That might work."

"I am sure it's not going to feel good, but it's our best shot," I said.

I turned Stella around while holding onto Lucas. Lucas grabbed Stella's mane and the back of the saddle. Stella did not move a muscle. I knew how much she loved Lucas. He bent his leg to put his knee and all of his weight into my locked hands and let out a loud, "SHIT!" Damn, I hated to see him hurt so bad. Tears started to sting my eyes, as I tried to will them away. I had to be strong now. No time to fall apart. In all the years I had known him, I had never seen him hurt this bad. Once he got his knee in my hands, he said, "Please hurry because this position really doesn't feel good."

"Okay, let's go. On three. One. Two. Three. Go."

I put everything I had into helping him up onto Stella, and at the same time, he tried to pull himself up as best he could with his swollen wrists. We managed to get him three-quarters of the way there, but he struggled to get his good leg over Stella. I gave it one more big push, as Stella took a step our way. That did it. Thank you, Stella. Lucas was on but had turned a terrible shade of grayish-white. He was hurting badly. I was starting to worry that he was going to pass out.

"Hey Lucas, let's take it slow, okay? We need to get down this hill first. Are you okay to start?"

"I think so."

I led Stella down that steep hill, stopping frequently to make sure that Lucas was okay. He did not look any better, but he was hanging in there. He seemed to wince more with every step. Once we were at the bottom, we just had to cross a short flat part and then back up a hill to our property. We were halfway there. I was starting to feel like we were going to make it.

"We're getting close Lucas. Hang in there."

All of a sudden, Stella stopped dead in her tracks. I looked at her and noticed the direction she was looking in off to her right. *Holy Crap! That damn lion has been following us!* There he was, silently stalking us. He was about fifteen yards away. Lucas saw him at the same time I did.

"Abby, where is your gun?" Lucas said calmly because I don't think he had it in him to use any more conviction.

"Right here. Do you want it? You are a much better shot, than me. Can you do it?"

"No. I can't shoot with my wrists. You have to do it. You can do it. Shoot that cat, Abby!"

Lucas was more pissed at that cat than anything else at that moment. I was scared that if I shot, Stella would jolt Lucas's leg. I also worried that if I missed, that damn cat would haunt us forever. Plus, we liked to ride our horses over here all the time and I was damned if that cat was going to put a stop to that. I was struggling between being scared, for so many reasons, and pissed that this cat was threatening us.

I aimed my gun, without my readers, while trying to hold onto Stella at the same time.

"Wait," said Lucas. "Let go of Stella. I have her. Use both hands and aim right behind and under his shoulder. Shoot to kill, Abby. Just like Sean taught you."

I let go of Stella, moved a few feet away, and aimed my gun again. *Oh, God. That damn cat is staring right at me as if it knows I won't pull the trigger. I have never killed anything, but that cat is looking right at me. What if she has babies? I don't even know if it is male or female. What if I just hurt it and it takes off? I know I cannot aim well without my reader glasses. Can I live with that?*

"That's it. Now take a deep breath, hold it, and pull the trigger. You've got this," Lucas was saying very calmly and quietly. I hesitated again. Lucas quietly, and more firmly said, "Abby, pull the fucking trigger!"

I held my breath, aimed where I was told, pulled the trigger, closed my eyes, and stopped breathing altogether.

When I opened my eyes, the lion was lying on the ground dead.

"I did it?" It was more of a question because I could not or did not want to believe it.

"Yes, you did. Great shot. It was a clean one. Now let's get home." Lucas urged, distracted by the pain in his leg and probably everywhere else.

I was somewhat in shock. I just shot and killed an animal for the first time in my life. I knew I had to do it, but it did not make me feel particularly good. So many emotions were going through me, I was overwhelmed and could feel tears welling up in my eyes. I wasn't even sure of the exact reason why. I am sure most of it was that I was so worried about my husband.

I looked over at Lucas. He looked very pale and like he would fall over any second. I began walking Stella up the hill to our property as quickly as I could, trying not to jostle Lucas too much while holding on to him at the same time. Once we got to the edge of our field, my parents and our neighbors, Katey and Scott, saw us and came rushing over to help.

· · · ● · ● · ● · · ·

We ended up in the emergency room for the rest of that day, getting Lucas's ankle x-rayed and surgery scheduled as well as having his ribs and his wrists x-rayed and a general once over to make sure he had no internal injuries. He had some badly bruised ribs, abrasions all over his side and the arm that he landed on, some cuts and scrapes on his face, a black eye, and two sprained wrists. Overall, he was pretty lucky.

While waiting for the results of his X-rays, Lucas asked me, "How did you get Stella to stomp her feet at that mountain lion?"

"I have no idea. That was all her. I just know she was trying to protect us as best as she could. In fact, I am one thousand percent sure she was."

"She did not back down either. Do you realize that?" asked Lucas.

"No, she didn't."

"Abby, do you realize how fast you came running up that hill?"

"No. I haven't really thought about it yet."

At that moment, that was the furthest thing from my mind. I was so worried about Lucas's injuries.

"And, I cannot believe you shot your gun from on top of her."

"Well, I did not see any other choice at that moment. I had to. I held on tight and pulled the trigger. Stella handled it well, didn't she?"

"I would say so."

"And, Abby, so did you. You stepped up, big time. I knew you were capable of all of that, and I am so thankful."

"You are welcome."

At that moment, what had transpired on those trails seemed like it had happened to somebody else. It couldn't have been me. The whole day seemed like it had been a dream—more like a nightmare, really. It just wasn't registering.

"Lucas?" the doctor asked, as he walked into the room with the X-rays in hand.

"I have your X-rays. Why don't we look at these together."

· · ● ● · ● ● · · ·

Lucas had surgery the next day on his ankle. Luckily, it had been a clean break, but it was badly displaced. He needed a few screws and a plate in it. He was so lucky he was not hurt worse.

To be fair, none of this was Diego's fault. The poor mule was traumatized. He was still young and had not gone on very many rides around there. It was going to take another year or two of riding him in these mountains regularly to get him over being spooked by new things. Lucas decided that at our ages, he preferred to have a horse that was already trained and had had all those rides. I thought that was a wonderful idea.

Not long after that, Lucas decided to sell Diego to a friend of ours who has a ranch with mostly mules. He uses them mainly to pack supplies in and out of the mountains for the Forest Service. He does ride them some too. From time to time, we go and visit Diego. He is thriving there with all the other mules.

Lucas has since found a very quiet-minded, young palomino that has been perfect and rarely spooks at anything. I am so relieved!

16

Recovery and Reflection

The day after Lucas's surgery, we returned home from the hospital. I got Lucas set up on the couch with pillows under his leg and an icepack, per the doctor's orders. I gave him one of his pain pills, insisting he take at least one. He was stubborn about taking medications. I got him some coffee. It was not yet time for lunch. Once he was settled, I asked, "Do you think you'll be okay if I go and grab a quick shower?"

"Of course," Lucas said, "take your time." Lucas was still a little out of it from the surgery. He seemed content to be able to catch up on the newly recorded *Dateline*.

"And, Abby," Lucas said, "thank you for everything. I still cannot believe you killed that cougar. You know, Abby, you are a much better rider than you think you are. I have always known that, which is why I would get so frustrated sometimes."

"Thanks," I replied, "and, I can't believe I did all of that either."

· · · **·** · **·** · · ·

I still had mixed emotions about that whole event. I was glad I was able to protect my family and that I had made a clean kill shot so as not to incur unnecessary suffering to the cat. I think I was lucky. I still didn't like the idea of killing an animal. Up until that moment, I had not had a chance to process everything that had unfolded over those last couple of days. We had been pretty busy with the emergency room, surgery the next day, and getting Lucas home and comfortable.

As I stepped into the warm shower, a surge of emotions seemed to overtake me, and a flood of tears started that I could not stop. I sat in the shower for about thirty minutes, quietly letting the tears flow while shaking uncontrollably. It was like a post-traumatic stress reaction to the recent events. I started thinking about my life in north Idaho over the last several years and realized how far I had come and how much I had grown as a person. I was not the same person I was when I left Virginia.

After remarrying an amazing man and moving 2,400 miles away from everything and everyone I had ever known to start a brand-new adventure and a completely different lifestyle in this beautiful, small agricultural county in north Idaho, not only had I gotten past the initial cultural shock of moving here, but I had embraced it. I found I preferred it and its laid-back outdoorsy lifestyle. Without realizing it, I had redefined my life.

I learned to horseback ride at forty-eight years old and overcame several mental blocks that were keeping me from progressing and gaining more confidence on a horse. This was a huge accomplishment for me. Since then, I have ridden my horses all over the mountains in north Idaho, and seen truly breathtaking places. With Copper and Stella, my confidence as a rider had grown exponentially.

I learned to shoot a gun and killed a mountain lion. While I will never like the idea of killing an animal, I knew that, if necessary, I was capable of defending myself and my family.

I had gotten to know some amazing people, especially women who are strong, intelligent, hard-working, and self-sufficient. They continued to amaze me. They were entirely different from my friends back on the East Coast. I have all the respect in the world for the women here and admired their strength and fortitude. They are truly remarkable women.

Seeing how happy and content people are with much less, was an eye-opener. I had always heard growing up that material stuff isn't important. However, people here live it and are some of the happiest people I know. It's more about the experiences, adventures, and relationships in life. It's what we do with our lives that is most important. I had seen some of the poorest people I know be the most helpful to others in need. It was heartwarming.

I had snowmobiled on the tops of the mountains and seen some unbelievably beautiful scenery. It was beautiful, exhilarating, and scary as hell. Some people call that living.

I had also found loyalty in the most unsuspecting places. Loyalty isn't just about staying faithful to a spouse, although that is the form I was most familiar with.

Lucas believed in me when I didn't believe in myself, whether it was running on a horse, shooting a mountain lion, or boldly trying a new career. He helped me find the courage to do things, even when I doubted myself. He showed me what commitment means. Although it took some time, he had allowed me to trust again.

I found love and loyalty with Copper, Toby, and Stella. Stella was ready to defend both Lucas and I against that mountain lion. She didn't spook and take off like a lot of horses or mules would have. She stayed with us, willing to do whatever we needed her to do. Her love and devotion to us was obvious and unwavering.

The sense of community I encountered while working with kids in 4-H, was truly impressive. The way families and local businesses came together to support these kids was unlike anything I could have imagined.

• • • ● • ● • • ● • •

Later that year, for my birthday and after Lucas recovered, he surprised me with a trip to the Oregon coast. He knew how much I had missed the beach. We went every summer when I lived in Virginia. In addition, one of my dreams had always been to run a horse on a beach. Lucas knew this too. However, in my mind it would forever be just a dream, not knowing how exactly we would do that.

We spent four days exploring the beaches and enjoying wonderful fresh seafood meals. The beaches were vastly different from the ones on the East Coast. There were houses on top of tall cliffs overlooking the shoreline with hundreds of steps leading down to the beach. There were huge rock formations scattered all over the beach—some even in the water. It was beautiful. We stayed in a quaint hotel overlooking a marina with seals constantly surfacing onto the docks. Every morning after breakfast, we would grab a coffee and walk all over that marina. There has always been something about being on the water that is so soothing and peaceful to me.

On our third day there, while driving along the coast, Lucas pulled into a horse property and parked the car.

"What are we doing, Lucas?"

"Well, you have always wanted to run a horse on the beach, so Happy Birthday."

"What? No way." I couldn't believe he was doing this. Immediately, my eyes filled with tears. "This may be the best birthday present of all time. Oh my gosh! Thank you."

We walked over to a small office in front of the barn and checked in. Next, we stood watching them bring out several horses, already tacked up and ready to go. One, in particular, caught our attention. He was huge, and when we asked, we were told he was a draft cross between a Belgian and a Percheron. His feet were as large as dinner plates. I couldn't believe they found a saddle that would fit him. I had only seen those draft horses pull wagons and things. I was sure our guide would be the one riding him. He was so majestic looking, it was hard to take your eyes off him.

Once all three horses were out of the barn, the trail guide called Lucas's name. He walked over and she introduced him to his horse, a normal-sized palomino with a very quiet demeanor.

"Abby?"

"Here," I said, walking over to her.

She walked over to that gigantic draft horse and said, "This is Texas. He is your horse."

"Wh...Wh...That's my horse?"

I looked over at Lucas, with a slight tinge of panic. He was grinning ear to ear and starting to laugh. *Holy Cow! That is a tremendous horse and I am going to be expected to run him on the beach. Oh my God!*

"Yep, step on around here. We have a mounting block for ya."

I needed all three steps on that mounting block to be able to climb on Texas. *Oh Lord, I hope he is quiet, or I will surely be dying on this beach today.* Lucas had arranged a private two-hour ride on the beach, just he and I and our guide specifically so we could run on the beach. They don't normally run the horses with larger groups.

As we walked the path to the beach, I thought this must be what it feels like to sit on top of an elephant. I was so high up, and the ground was so far down. At the same time, I was thrilled to be riding a horse on the beach, and a draft horse at that.

It was an overcast day and there were no other people on the beach. The ocean seemed calmer than I would have expected. It was a comfortable seventy-two degrees. There was a slight breeze coming off the ocean. I have always loved the smell of salt water at the beach. It reminds me of my childhood trips to the beach, which are some of my favorite memories. I was currently sitting on a horse on a beach—two of my favorite things in the world. I was in heaven!

We walked down toward the water and then along the beach in the harder-packed wet sand. We walked for about five minutes before the guide, who was in front of us, said, "Are you ready to run?"

I looked at Lucas and gave him a little grimace. Lucas, immediately sensing my fear of being on a taller horse, looked at me and said, "You have got to be kidding. Abby, you've got this." With that, he hollered, "Yes, we are ready."

The guide cued her horse into a run. Lucas's horse did a little buck but then went right into a run. My turn. I cursed at that stupid fear in my head, took a deep breath, and spurred Texas into a run.

As soon as Texas had taken several long strides, I felt so much more comfortable and started laughing loudly and hollering, "Oh my gosh, this is awesome!"

For being such a large draft horse, Texas had the most comfortable run ever. We must have run for close to a mile through the surf before stopping to give the horses a rest. We walked a little and then ran again. This was the best birthday ever! I wanted to remember every second of this day and didn't want it to ever end. Toward the end of the ride, we stopped to let our guide take some photos of us while we stood in front of a couple of big rock formations in the ocean. While sitting on Texas in the surf and looking out at the ocean, I felt like a Viking woman warrior. I had run on a horse on the beach and not just any horse, a draft horse. This day was priceless.

· · · ● · ● · · · ·

So many times, I have thought about how close I came to missing out on this beautiful life with an even more special man. If I had turned around that night in Lucas's driveway and gone home, we never would have gotten married or moved across the country. If I had given in to my fear, I would have missed out on some of my best years. Instead, I chose to trust.

The biggest lesson I learned in years since meeting Lucas, and largely due to Lucas continuously pushing me outside of my comfort zone, is this: in this fast-paced world, time goes by quickly. Most are so busy with careers and raising kids that they tend to get complacent in their daily lives, only to arrive at old age with regrets of things they have not done or at least attempted. It is best to have the confidence and courage to try new things, whether it is moving 2,400 miles away, changing the focus of a career, or volunteering for new things, embracing both successes and failures. Both are important and will propel one to the next adventure in life. Keeping an open mind, and more importantly, a sense of humor is key when taking that leap and living life to its fullest. After all, it is often the things in life that seem the scariest that often bring us the greatest rewards.

Life with Lucas was never going to be boring. Our adventures are just getting started.

Epilogue

We have been living in north Idaho for a little over four years now. I may be starting to acclimate to this lifestyle, a little. Since leaving my 4-H position, Lucas and I have been contemplating if I should keep working in real estate or if he and I should do something together. Lucas seems more than ready for a new adventure.

I am feeling a little more confident in a farming community. I have actually found that I enjoy physical farm work and find it incredibly satisfying at the end of the day. I have had several ideas, including a dairy goat farm, focusing on goat milk ice cream. Apparently, many people who are lactose intolerant, seem to have no problem drinking goat's milk. Yet, I could not find any goat's milk ice cream anywhere in north Idaho. There did not seem to be any real competition in this area. Lucas did not like it. He kept saying he could not see me getting up early every morning and milking all the goats and then doing it again every night.

I threw out the idea of starting an alpaca farm. I researched it and even went to visit another alpaca farm in the area. The money is really made in the breeding, not the wool. Lucas did not like that idea much either. He thought it was more of a fad thing, and that we would end up losing money. In addition, I would have to drive all over the country taking our alpacas to alpaca shows. Maybe he is right about that one.

I then suggested we try homesteading. We may not make much money doing that, but we will not be spending much either. He looked at me funny, as if doubting my ability to truly do this, and said, "If you are serious about that, write down your definition of homesteading and outline a business plan."

So, I sat down and wrote him a letter with my proposal. The following is that letter, along with his responses throughout, which he sent back to me.

Dear Husband,

You asked me to write down what my idea of homesteading is. It is something I have wanted to try and we have been discussing since moving from Washington, DC to this small little town in the mountains near the Canadian border of north Idaho years ago. We wanted a more rural, laid-back lifestyle, and I was tired of the fast-paced corporate sales world I had been in for thirty years. I look at homesteading as something of a personal challenge. I also think, worst case, it will save us some money and we may learn a few things—not to mention all the time we can spend together since you are already retired. I think we should agree to do this for one year. Of course, if it works well, we can always do it indefinitely. Writing it down is forcing me to think it through. So, here goes.

We grow and preserve all our own veggies and potatoes, etc. We can or freeze most of them. Since our garden was a complete failure because we have nothing but sand as far down as you can dig on our property, and no amount of organic matter (I am convinced) is going to make a difference in our lifetime, and the so-called garden is now the chicken run, we will need to purchase all of our veggies and potatoes at the farmers' market when in season and preserve them.

Are you crazy? Why would we pay for these, spend money canning them, and all the labor when we could just buy them when we need them? It would be foolish to spend the same or more to can purchased produce.

Since we don't have fruit trees...we can purchase local fruit when in season at the farmers' markets and preserve it—can or freeze it. Luckily, we have planted about seventy various berry bushes.

Are you crazy? Makes no sense.

No TV. We give this up. Save the money and find other ways to amuse ourselves.

Hunt for elk and fowl (guinea hens, pheasant, duck, etc.). I think I could hunt for fowl...I just don't want any part of killing a larger animal, i.e., elk. I would need one of those camo outfits and some of that black stuff the football players put under their eyes to smear my face with. Oh and, a small gun but large enough to take out a bird. That could be fun. We could even build one of those duck blinds.

We don't have guinea hens, ducks, or pheasants. We have turkeys and grouse. For a trial run, I will kill several and leave them in the sink for you. Let's start by seeing how that goes.

We will need to purchase one hog for pork. Raising our own hog will ensure it is free from added hormones, antibiotics, etc. It is a little more organic. I wonder what would happen if we raised the hog in the same pen alongside the chickens?

We have chickens, so we have plenty of eggs. We could add some meat chickens to our group to subsidize our hunting efforts.

Already costing us more than buying, not to mention clogging my arteries.

We should also try foraging for herbs, mushrooms, and medicinal plants. We will need to read up on these. I am sure it will be very enlightening. We have about seventy wooded acres. I know we have lots of rosehips on our property. They are loaded with vitamin C. We can dry them and make them into tea. At least we won't get scurvy. My only fear is that we will accidentally ingest or touch something harmful, which will cause illness or horrible rashes. We now know how prone I am to rashes in the mountains of this part of the country. We may want to focus on the medicinal plants first. We also have tons of huckleberries close by. Huckleberry daiquiris help the rashes feel better.

You will need to drink the huckleberry daiquiris to offset the weight loss from not eating the mushrooms. You hate them.

We will have to purchase a few essentials: flour, sugar, oatmeal, coffee, baking powder/soda, salt, pepper, etc. But, maybe we only buy a specific amount for the year and make it last.

Also, make-up and hair products are essential. After all, I do still want to be married at the end of this adventure. I will, however, give up pedicures, and I don't care about manicures.

We purchase one dairy cow for milk, butter, etc. I suppose we will need to purchase a few glass milk jugs, and could you make me one of those little three-legged stools to sit on while I milk the cow in the mornings? Do you think the dairy cow would be okay in with the chickens and hog? The cow and hog may help keep the hawks out of there. I should be able to churn butter and make cheese with some of the milk also.

Loren, our neighbor, has a cow. I will call him and tell him that you are willing to do the milking duties for a week or so to see how you like it. Do you prefer the morning (5:30 a.m.) or the evening? Doing both might really give you a good feel for it.

Fish – we can do this together! I like trout and salmon. I think we should set up a drying rack behind the house so we can dry some salmon, just like they do on that Alaska show you like to watch.

We learn to make bread and do it!

Hang all clothes on the line to dry outside during good weather. We will still use the washing machine, but we could make our soap from the fat of our slaughtered hog. Using as many parts of the animal as we can is homesteading at its best. Of course, we will need to use the dryer in the winter months. We can also give up dryer sheets.

Let's not forget: no eating out, no buying premade sandwiches, and we give up Facebook (just wouldn't be homesteading with Facebook). No bottled water (or store-bought water). No premade food (pizzas, chicken strips, pancake mix, cornbread mix, salad dressings, prepackaged spices, like chili mixes, etc.) We also make our yogurt....

Abby, are you out of your mind?

· · · **·** · **·** · · · ·

Later that evening as we were enjoying soaking in the hot tub, we were discussing the pros and cons of homesteading.

"I feel it is something we can do. Let's just agree to do it for one year, no more, no less, and see how that goes," I suggested.

"Abby, okay. If you really want to do this, I will build you a garden with raised beds and a greenhouse. I will also put together a proper chicken coop. We can get a few animals. Before we embark on this, however, we are going to have to discuss who will be responsible for what."

"That is fine. I am totally up for the challenge."

Four years earlier, after just arriving in Idaho, I would have never, in a million years, seen myself doing something like this. Now, it is something of a personal challenge that Lucas and I could do together. With him by my side, I believed we could do anything we put our minds to.

"Okay."

"Okay?"

"Yes. This should be interesting," muttered Lucas, as he gave me that same smug grin he had given me when he asked me to help breast some geese several years earlier.

At that exact moment, I felt so relaxed and content with our lives. It was a cold, clear late fall evening, perfect for sitting in the hot tub. There were millions of stars in the sky. We could even see what I thought must have been the Milky Way. When out of nowhere, SPLASH!!!

Something big had jumped into the middle of the hot tub with us. I screamed and jumped up. *Oh my God! What is that big dark thing in the water next to us?*

In an instant, I realized it was Red, the cat. He was scrambling to get out, as I quickly and clumsily reached over to give him a toss out of the hot tub.

"Didn't that scare the crap out of you, Lucas?" I asked as I stood there catching my breath.

"Not really." He never even flinched.

My next thought as I looked at Lucas, was that it was freezing out, and that cat was now soaked. He was going to freeze.

I grabbed my towel, jumped out of the hot tub, and started chasing the cat around the backyard and porch. He was now skittish after just being traumatized. Since he is a longer-haired cat, he also looked like he had just been electrocuted, with his hair standing straight up in spikes on his head. He ran under the table we used to eat from in the summer, which had a vinyl cover over it.

It is not until I was on my hands and knees, halfway under this table with the towel in my hand, that I realized I was buck naked. I cringed. *Oh God! I am sure Lucas is totally amused by this whole scene.*

Let the next adventure begin!

Many thanks to:

My parents for always encouraging and cheering me on. I would not be here without you.

Joe Gilbert, my coach. This endeavor would not have been possible without his endless knowledge and direction.

My editor, Susan Michaud. You gave me confidence to move forward with this book.

My many beta readers, including Nancy Brosnahan, Kris Kwickwire, Mary Beck, Debbie Foersch, Anne Talbott, Carolyn Birrell, Dawn Hansen, Angie Wilkinson, Jackie Delclos, Theresa Liakopoulos, Jennifer Johnson, and Donna Eichna.

Melanie Geaslin, for proofing the final version and sharing her wisdom.

Rich Feickert, again, thank you for being understanding while this project consumed most of my time this past winter.

This book would not have been possible without any of you.